The DYNAMIC Trio

Bill Stewart

The Life Changing Power
of Hope, Faith and Love

THE DYNAMIC TRIO
Copyright © 2016 by Bill Stewart

Printed in Canada

ISBN: 978-1-4866-1172-0

Word Alive Press
131 Cordite Road, Winnipeg, MB R3W 1S1
www.wordalivepress.ca

Cataloguing in Publication may be obtained through Library and Archives Canada

In memory of my father and mother,
Robert and Annie Stewart—good people

Contents

SECTION I
Hope: The Architect

CHAPTER ONE

THE BABY

My name is Allison, and I'm twenty years old. I'm just emerging from my teenage years, and they've been difficult years full of turmoil and conflict. While it's quite common for girls of this age to be unsettled, I think it was worse for me because six years ago my mother died. My mother and I were very close. She'd always been a good, steady influence in my life, and she would have understood better what it's like for a girl to be emerging into womanhood. I say "better" in the sense that she would have understood better than does my father, who is a very fine man, but has little understanding about the passionate emotions and changeable needs of a teenage girl. Although my father tried his best to help me make the stormy transition into womanhood, I felt I was very much alone. I had to find my own way through all of the explosive and contradictory issues that confront a girl who has developed the body of a woman but still has many of the emotions and feelings of a child. I desperately needed the understanding, companionship and strength of a compassionate mother, but I didn't have it. So I had to grow up on my own.

I have to confess that I did not do a very good job of growing up. I got into the wrong company, and I was subject to erratic mood swings. I went through periods of wild hilarity and other periods of sullen depression. There were some really good times but they were overshadowed by some really bad times. While my friends were very important to me, they weren't a good influence, and they led me into things I would never have ventured into on my own. In order to please them and be with them, I became someone whom I did not like and I acted in ways that left me feeling uncomfortable.

As a teenager, I experienced the ecstasy of falling madly in love and the agony of falling out of it—a few times. I wanted the freedom and authority of being an adult, but didn't know how to handle this freedom in a responsible way. I tended to confuse my freedom with license. In my uncertainty, I crossed some behavioural lines and did things I never should have done. In the name of "being myself," I got into activities that I know would have grieved my mother.

During these years, my relationship with my father was very rocky. I needed someone to tell me what the lines and restrictions were, but when my father tried to guide and discipline me I rebelled against him angrily. I resented any guidance or direction he gave me. He just didn't understand. There were times when I felt great appreciation for my father, and other times when I felt I almost hated him. Even though we lived in the same house, we seemed to exist in different worlds. We could not communicate. Any attempt at communication was short, tense, and often ended up in a shouting match or with me in tears.

My father is a successful man. He's an architect with his own business that he started up a few years ago, but he's very absorbed in his work. He has just won a large contract to design a major conference centre in the expensive downtown part of the city. This is an important assignment for him, and if he does well at it, it should open up many other lucrative opportunities. The success in Father's business life, however, does not translate into happiness in his home and personal life. I think, he deeply misses my mother. He seems lonely, empty, and a little lost without her. Since her death, I've certainly added to his problems. By no means have I been a comfort and support to him in his grief. In our times of conflict, he often says, "Your mother would not approve of this," or even more often, "I just don't know what to do with you."

Fortunately, my wild social life didn't destroy my schoolwork. I was able to graduate from high school, and I'm now in my second year at university. I have vague hopes of becoming an optometrist, but everything is confused right now and I don't know what I'll end up doing.

Something then happened that brought my wild ways to a dramatic and sudden halt. I got pregnant. The man who I thought was the father of the child refused to take any responsibility and disappeared from my life. I was alone and suddenly carrying a weight of responsibility I didn't want. When news of my condition leaked out to my friends, they all seemed to retreat and distance themselves from me instead of rallying around and supporting me. Apparently I wasn't fun to be with anymore. They were sorry for me, but they didn't want to spoil their fun by having someone around who had major problems. It was as if I'd suddenly caught a contagious disease. A horror of depression and discouragement came over me. Things got so bad I even contemplated suicide. One night, trembling with anxiety, I got into a bath with a razor, planning to cut my wrists and end it all. When the time came to do the act, however, I didn't have the courage.

In my turmoil, I knew I had to confide in my father. One night at the supper table I broke the news.

"Father, I hate to tell you this, but I'm pregnant."

Supper was forgotten. We sat and talked. I knew he was deeply distressed and disappointed. This was not the way he'd dreamed his little girl would turn out. He did, however, confirm what was in my mind already—I would need to get an abortion.

"A baby now would destroy all of your plans and your prospects. Besides," he added with a gesture that indicated his despair, "how could we properly take care of a baby in our house?"

He was right. A baby would change everything, and I wanted freedom to pursue my career, whatever it was going to be. I knew the time would come in my life when I'd want to have a baby, but not yet. Not under these circumstances. I wasn't ready for motherhood—financially or emotionally. I understood that at this point in my life I couldn't provide a baby with the security and care that it needed. Besides, I didn't want to be saddled with the responsibilities and restrictions that a baby would bring. In my mind, I acccepted that an abortion made good sense. My problem was that while I agreed with the reasoning of my mind, the emotions and natural instincts of my heart wouldn't follow the lead of my mind. I could see that aborting the pregnancy was the sensible thing to do, but my heart and my conscience were not agreeing with this conclusion. I wanted to keep my baby. I wanted to love and care for it. The inner conflict was tearing me apart. I made another attempt at suicide, but once again I didn't have the courage to follow through.

In the midst of this confusion, my father really did help me. He wasn't in conflict about what should be done. He made arrangements with a doctor, who in turn made arrangements with the hospital. In a whirlwind of decisions and activity, I found myself in the hospital with the abortion successfully completed. The medical procedure had gone as planned with no complications. I had had the abortion. The baby was gone and supposedly my problems were solved. The abortion itself had seemed a fairly simple and easy procedure. It was soon over and I was released from hospital to go home and get on with my life. But while the physical aspect of the abortion was rather easy and simple, I found the internal conflict was far from over. I was guilt ridden and full of regrets and questions about what I had done.

After the abortion, I fell into a period of deep depression. Thoughts of suicide kept suggesting themselves to me. But while I gave it serious thought I never had the courage to actually do the act. My father remained consistent and strong. He continued to assure me that I'd done the right thing. When I told him of my inner conflict over the abortion, he said quite confidently that these emotions would pass and I would be fine. I hoped he was right, but at that moment "these emotions" were not passing.

Even in the depth of my depression, I became aware that the abortion had changed a number of things. First, I lost my taste for my former wild and undisciplined social life. It now held no appeal for me. I wanted something else. I knew I had to get my values and priorities straightened out and map out for myself a course in life that was quite different from the one I'd been following. I didn't know what that course would be, but I knew that my old way of life would no longer satisfy me or bring the peace and contentment I longed for.

Secondly, my friends changed. My previous friends seemed to disappear; they didn't come around anymore. I stopped receiving invitations to parties and nights out. I admit that some of them did make halfhearted attempts get me back into the swing of things, but I turned them down and they didn't ask again. I realized that they belonged to another world that I wasn't part of ... nor did I want to be. The problem was that while I had lost all of my previous friends and social interests, I didn't have anything else to put in their place. I was lonely, hungry for life, and looking for something, but I didn't know what it was, so I continued to be depressed and lost.

One positive change after the abortion concerned my relationship with my father. He did seem to have some understanding of the conflict and loss I was experiencing, but he remained confident and assured that I had done the right thing. At this point, I greatly needed his support and respect, and he was beginning to reach out to me and give me some consolation without blame and condemnation. Although I was too proud to admit it to him, I really appreciated this and began to rely on his strength and assurance.

The most important change I experienced after the abortion, however, was that after the loss of my old acquaintances, I began to long for some new friends. There was one girl in particular that I became aware of. Her name was Karen, and she attended some of the same classes as I at the university. I'd noticed her before, but at that time we seemed to have very little in common and never approached one another. She was just not part of my circle. Karen, however, seemed to have heard about my problems and started going out of her way to make contact with me. She offered friendship, and in my loneliness and confusion I was more than willing to respond to her. More than anyone else, Karen seemed to understand and care. We often ate lunch together at school, and we phoned each other a lot. We also went for long walks. I was able to unburden myself to Karen. I felt safe and comfortable in her friendship, and she in turn seemed to enjoy my company. With the passage of time, we became good friends.

One day, while on one of our walks, our friendship rose to a new level of confidence and trust. Although I didn't know it at that time, the direction of my life began to change that day. As we walked, Karen felt free to confide in me.

"You know Allison," she began in a rather strained and tentative voice, "I understand what you're going through with this abortion, because I was pregnant too."

I was so stunned I couldn't speak.

"When I found out I was pregnant," she continued, "my whole world collapsed. This wasn't supposed to happen to me."

I understood this completely but still could not make any comment.

"My decision as to what to do about it, however, was different from yours. I decided to have the baby. He was a boy, and I called him Jimmy. Instead of keeping him, though, I decided to adopt him out." With a tremor in her voice, Karen continued. "It was heart wrenching, but I knew my precious baby boy would be in good hands. The adoptive parents couldn't conceive, and they wanted a child desperately. I knew they'd love Jimmy and care for him. They were also financially secure, so my boy would have good prospects and opportunities. I knew they could provide much more for him than I could ever hope to do. And for me? It enabled me to pick up the pieces of my life, get on with my studies, and prepare for a career and a life of my own. It's been a struggle, but I've learned to accept the situation. I'm now comfortable with the decisions I made and I'm at peace. I know little Jimmy is secure and well taken care of. I'm working for a future; I have hopes and purposes. I'm no longer lost or depressed, but I can see where I want to go and I'm working towards it."

I was absorbed in Karen's story, but I interrupted her and said rather desperately: "I'm not there, and I don't have peace. I don't think of the future; I only think of the past. My past failures and foolishness haunt me all the time. I'm plagued with guilt and sorrow over how I've lived and the dreadful consequences it's brought. I don't know what to make of the future. I don't know where I'm going or what I'm supposed to do. I'm lost. You talk of purpose, but I don't know the purpose of my life. I seem to have made such a mess of things; I'm sinking in the mess, and I don't know how to get out of it."

Karen turned and looked me straight in the eye.

"Allison, do you know what you need? What you need is some hope."

I didn't know it then, but those words were going to change everything.

"Hope?" I replied. "What in all the world has hope got to do with it?"

"Hope has everything to do with it. You're acting as if nothing good is going to happen and nothing worthwhile lies ahead. You want to commit suicide because you think there's nothing worth living for. You have no prospects for the future, only a past that you're sorry about and a present in which you're lost. You're in a dark room with no light getting in at all. Hope, Allison, can bring a ray of light into that darkness, and you'll begin to see things that you've lost sight of."

I looked at Karen and could tell that she was sincere about what she was saying. She really believed it.

"But," I said, "I don't understand, how hope can help me."

"You know," Karen responded, "my pastor at church spoke about hope last Sunday. He said hope was about the future. Hope tells us that good things are going to happen, and great things are still to be accomplished. When you have hope, you believe good things are ahead. He explained that when we're filled with hope, we stand on tiptoe with excitement and reach out to the future with anticipation.

"It sounds rather idealistic to me," I replied with some skepticism.

"But Allison, you need something. You need help. Hope would tell you that you have a purpose and a meaning. All is not lost. Good things— great things—can still be ahead of you. Believe that and your darkness will begin to fade and the future will take on a very different colour."

I didn't want to discourage my new friend, so I replied doubtfully.

"Well, it sounds good, but isn't it a little unrealistic, a bit like 'pie in the sky by and by?'"

We continued to walk in thoughtful silence. Finally, Karen ventured an invitation.

"A group of us meet every Tuesday evening for a Bible study. We enjoy one another's company, and there's good, open, friendly discussion about some things in the Bible. The group is made up mostly of younger people. Some are married and some are single, but we mix well. Our pastor indicated to the congregation on Sunday that he was going to take a few weeks and speak to us about the three great Christian characteristics of hope, faith and love. He began on Sunday morning by speaking about hope and it sounded very exciting to us in the group. We asked him if he would attend our Bible study so that we could discuss with him the meaning of these three dominant Christian virtues. He agreed and will be coming next Tuesday to talk about hope. Why don't you come and be part of that discussion?"

I was very hesitant. "Oh, I don't know about that. I'm not very religious and haven't gone to church much, so I don't know anything about these things. I don't know how I'd fit in with a religious group; it's just not where I've been in life."

"I think you'll enjoy this group," persisted Karen. "They're all about our age or a little older. They won't preach at you. Your ideas will be accepted. Besides, it's not all serious stuff; we have fun together, too. It'll be good for you, and it may give you some direction on how to move ahead with your life."

"But I don't want to confide in a group of strangers about all of my problems," I explained.

"You won't have to. Nobody will know about your abortion or your contemplated suicide; they'll simply accept you as you are."

I still wasn't convinced, so Karen put it very wisely.

"I'll pick you up next Tuesday and take you to the group. If you don't want to go, let me know and I won't bother to pick you up."

This left the decision in my hands. Over the next few days I thought seriously about her invitation. It certainly couldn't do any harm, and it may introduce me to a group of new friends. I was certainly hungry for that. I thought about hope and "reaching into the future with excitement."

I knew that kind of attitude was certainly a long way from where I was at the moment. Maybe there was more to this hope thing than I thought. I decided to give it a try, so on Tuesday evening Karen arrived and we went together to my very first Bible study group.

CHAPTER TWO

THE FRIENDS

Tuesday arrived and Karen picked me up as promised. On the way to the Bible study, there were some questions I wanted to ask.

"I've never been to a Bible study group before," I said. "What happens? How many people will be there? Will I have to say anything? They won't preach at me will they?"

Karen smiled at my anxieties.

"Usually there are about twelve to fifteen of us," she replied. "Tonight, since the pastor will be here, there may be more people turn up. We meet in the family room, and there will be coffee and tea available. We sit and chat for a while, which is always very pleasant. After about fifteen minutes, the leader calls us together and we begin the Bible study. Tonight the pastor will be leading us. He'll talk to us about hope and faith and love. There will be plenty of questions and discussion, but you only need to speak if you wish to. But you should feel free to ask questions or make comments. The whole thing will last about an hour and a half to two hours. We often close with a time of prayer."

"Prayer!" I exclaimed in a bit of a panic. "They won't ask me to pray, will they?"

Karen laughed at my discomfort. "No! You can be sure they'll not ask you to pray. I think this is going to help you, Allison," she said seriously. "This group has been a great help to me. They're not going to judge you, criticize you, preach at you, or pry into your personal life. You'll find that most of us have problems of our own that we're working our way through. We help each other and support one another. They'll reach out to you, accept you, and include you in the group."

I appreciated Karen's assurances, but I was still rather apprehensive. After all, I was an outsider going into an established group of people who were friends and who were familiar with each other. They were going to be talking about subjects to which I had never given serious consideration, and I'd be in a setting that was strange to me. Religion hadn't been important in our home.

I expressed my concerns to Karen. "You know, I'm not comfortable with this. Religion just hasn't been part of my life. I just don't know what I'm getting into."

Karen reached over and patted me on the shoulder.

"I know, but remember that I'll be there with you, and I really expect that you'll fit in very well. I think you'll enjoy these people. Look," she pointed, "here's the house we're going to. It belongs to Jim and Carol Dexter. He's a bank manager, and she works in a beauty parlor. They have a nice large family room in their basement, which is why we meet here. There's plenty of room for us all, and they also own a piano, which helps when we sing."

There were already a number of cars parked around the house, so I knew we weren't the first ones there. In response to our knock at the door, a lady, who I assumed was Carol Dexter, welcomed us. She was very gracious and pleasant, and after taking our coats she led us downstairs to the family room. I could hear a buzz of noise; the conversation and laughter created a friendly and warm atmosphere.

Since I was new to the group, Carol took me around and introduced me to everyone. Karen tagged along for support. I met four married couples, a few single ladies, and three single men. One of the men was introduced to me as Kyle. His handshake was firm and warm, and his eyes sparkled with life. He had a ready smile, and he seemed open and friendly.

"Allison, I'm glad to meet you," he said.

I sensed his sincerity, and my tension began to ease a little. Finally Carol introduced me to the pastor, whom she called Pastor Lindsey. He too was warm and sincere when he shook my hand and welcomed me. Pastor Lindsey looked to be in his late forties, making him the oldest in the group. Carol was probably in her early forties, but the rest of the group was younger and in their twenties or thirties. Everyone stood around in small clusters talking and laughing and clearly enjoying one another. They were not at all what I expected from a group of religious people. I'd expected them to be rather solemn, serious, and probably a little old fashioned. This group did not fit into that picture at all.

After completing the introductions, Carol gave me a cup of coffee and told me to make myself at home before moving on to speak with some of the others. I'd hardly finished stirring the milk into my coffee when Kyle came over and joined Karen and me. He looked to be about my age, but was tall with a rather unruly head of brown hair. His smile was captivating and friendly.

"So," he said by way of opening the conversation, "you two are going to school together?"

We both nodded.

"I know what Karen is studying," he said as he turned to me, "but what are you into?"

I explained that Karen and I were taking similar courses, and that I hoped to get into optometry.

"Good," Kyle enthused. "I'm studying engineering, and if I ever get through it, that's what I hope to be."

With the social ice broken we stood and chatted for a few minutes until I noticed a rather dignified man coming down the stairs. Karen leaned over and whispered, "That's Jim Dexter, Carol's husband. He's usually the leader of the group." Jim stood on the final step, raised his voice, and spoke above the murmur of general conversation.

"Why don't you find yourselves a seat," he suggested, "and we'll get started."

Kyle took charge of Karen and me and guided us to a broad chesterfield where the three of us sat down with Kyle in the middle of us both. It was a comfortable place to sit. I was beginning to relax and anticipate the evening.

When everyone had settled and made themselves at ease, Jim opened the meeting.

"I want to welcome everyone tonight. We especially want to acknowledge some people who've never been here before and give them a special welcome."

Jim pointed out one of the married couples as new to the group and also one of the single ladies. He then looked at me and introduced me as Karen's friend. Everyone clapped and smiled at the introductions. It all seemed warm and informal, and I felt accepted.

"We're very glad to have Pastor Lindsey here tonight," Jim continued as heads nodded in agreement. "Those of you who were at church recently heard that he's going to be preaching about hope, faith, and love for a few weeks. Because the subject is so important to us and vital to the growth of our Christian walk with God, I thought it would be fitting to have him come to our group and discuss the subject with us for a few weeks. He graciously accepted the invitation. I'm going to hand the meeting over to him at this time and assure him that we're anxious to learn and understand more about these vital Christian virtues."

Pastor Lindsey remained seated, but he leaned forward and expressed his pleasure at being there and stated that he hoped that the few sessions together would be helpful to us all. He had a deep, rich voice that had a firmness and authority to it. I listened with interest as he began.

"A few years ago, I was doing some mountain climbing in the Canadian Rockies. I remember vividly the day I climbed Mount Rundle in Banff National Park. To stand on top of any of these great mountains is a wonderful experience. That day on the top of Mount Rundle the weather was unusually clear and bright. In the clearness I could see innumerable snow covered peaks stretching out into the distance. As I looked towards the north and the west, the massive Rocky Mountains seemed to stretch into infinity, but when I looked southeast, I could immediately see one mountain that stood out against all of the others. What I was seeing was the towering strength of Mt. Assiniboine. It reached up above all of the other peaks around it. It's a grand pyramid of sheer rock ... majestic and dominant. I could understand why it had been called the Matterhorn of the Rockies. It was a very impressive sight."

As the pastor said all of this I thought, *He's into mountain climbing. I'm surprised. I thought most pastors were bookish, armchair types of people.*

"I thought of that experience when I started to prepare this series about hope, faith, and love," he continued. "Many Christian virtues reach up and point us to God and His way of life, but the ones that tower above the rest, like Mount Assiniboine, the qualities that stand out in their grandeur and their importance, are hope, faith, and love. They are predominant. If you're an earnest soul seeking to experience what a Christ-like life is like, then you'll understand that these three qualities are the most vital ingredients for that kind of life. No Christian experience will flourish without them. No fellowship with God will be complete if they are absent.

No one can meaningfully be a follower of Christ and neglect the development of hope, faith, and love in their lives. As we talk together about these qualities, it's essential that you realize just how vital they are to the richness of your maturing walk with God. In short, we cannot expect to live fruitfully and effectively for Christ without these qualities. In this time together, I want you to understand what these qualities are and how they function in your life."

This sounds good, I thought, *but I don't see how it's going to help me get over my abortion and stop being depressed and discouraged.*

It was as if the pastor had heard me say these words.

"I also want you to understand," he continued, "that the development of these qualities will impact how you deal with all of life—not just the spiritual part. They will affect how you feel, how you make decisions, how you plan for your future, how you set your priorities, and how you interact with other people. Hope, faith, and love will have a dynamic and powerful influence on the formation of your personality and character. They'll give guidance and direction as you seek to fulfill your purpose and discover God's will for your life. When they're present in your life, you'll be an entirely different person. They are the outstanding Christian virtues and the central qualities of the Christian character. More than anything else, they're what people should see when they look at our lives and personalities. They are the dynamic trio—hope and faith and love."

He's certainly promising a lot, I thought. *Could hope, faith, and love really make that much difference in my life? I've never given them much thought before.*

"Right from the beginning," continued Pastor Lindsey, "I want you to see that they operate as a trio ... a dynamic trio. They sing together. They harmonize with each other. They support and encourage one another. You can't be strong in love and weak in hope and faith. You can't be bright with hope but lacking in faith and love. Hope, faith, and love do not do well as soloists, but they are dynamic as a trio. I want you to connect the three together. Often in the Bible these three qualities are grouped together as a co-operating unit." He picked up his Bible and referring to it said, "The apostle Paul joins them together when he says in 1 Corinthians thirteen, verse thirteen: *'And now these three remain; faith, hope and love. But the greatest of these is love.'* They work in harmony together. They're not soloists; they're a trio. Paul grouped them together again in 1 Thessalonians one, verse three where he says, *'We remember before our God and Father your work produced by faith, your labor prompted by love, and your endurance inspired by hope in our Lord Jesus Christ.'*

"In chapter five, verse eight of that same book Paul describes the Christian life as warfare against the evil in the world, and he explains how important faith, hope, and love are if we are to be victorious in this war. He says, *'But since we belong to the day, let us be sober, putting on faith and love as a breastplate, and the hope of salvation as a helmet.'* As you can see, the three great qualities work together and harmonize with each other. One cannot flourish without the other."

"As I see it," said one of the ladies, "it would be like growing a healthy garden. A garden needs three things if it's to grow to maturity. It needs sun, soil, and water, and it needs them all in balance. If it gets sun and water but has no soil, then it cannot grow. If it has sun and soil but no water, then it doesn't grow. To be a fruitful garden, you need all three and in the proper mixture. If I understand you correctly, Pastor, you're saying that if we're to be truly fruitful in our Christian lives, we'll need to have hope, faith, and love functioning in a balanced fashion. "Well said," replied the pastor. "That's a good illustration of how the three qualities harmonize together. In fact, if I'm not mistaken, I believe a lot of the energy that the Holy Spirit is pouring into your life right now is devoted to getting you to accept, understand, and experience these three great qualities. One of the great objectives of the Holy Spirit is to fill your life with hope and faith and love. All three are essential: hope without faith and love is wishful thinking and empty daydreaming. Faith without hope and love is blind and empty activity. Love without hope and faith is shallow sentimentality."

Could that be true? I wondered. Does God really want to fill me with hope, faith, and love? I certainly can see how my life would be different if I had more of them. In fact, the way I've been living, they've been noticeable by their absence. But how do I get them? Do I get them from God?

The pastor paused to see if anyone else wanted to make a comment, but I wasn't brave enough to give voice to my thoughts. No one else spoke up, so he continued.

"So that's the first thought I want you to get. They work together as a cooperating unit. They are a dynamic trio—hope and faith and love."

CHAPTER THREE

THE FUTURE

When Pastor Lindsey seemed satisfied that we all understood the relationship between the three qualities, so he continued.

"Let's begin by talking about hope. Hope deals with the future. It's an attitude towards the future. Hope is the happy anticipation that good things are still to come, the exciting expectation that good things are going to happen. Hope is the stimulating challenge that worthwhile things have yet to be attained, accomplished, and experienced."

The pastor looked at his notes. "The dictionary defines hope as 'entertaining the expectation of something desired.' Another dictionary defines hope as 'desire with the expectation of fulfillment.'

"There are a number of things in these definitions I want to point out to you so that we have a good understanding of what we really mean by hope. First, I want you to see that hope is something that's 'entertained.' We can entertain thoughts of hope like we entertain guests in our home. If they're warmly received and made comfortable, then they'll be glad to come back again. If we're neglectful and thoughtless, then the guests may not be anxious to return. The same applies to hope. We accept it and welcome it into our thoughts. Hope can be deliberately cultivated. It's an attitude that can be encouraged and developed ... we entertain it. Alternatively, we can neglect it, crush it, and doubt it. If we do this, then the power and strength of hope are weakened. It's very much a matter of personal choice whether we open our arms and embrace hope or turn our back on it."

The pastor let us think about that for a moment or two and then quietly continued. "One of the decisions that I hope you'll all make during these classes is to deliberately start entertaining your hopes. Make room for them, accept them, give them attention and care so that they flourish and grow and thrive in your mind and heart. Welcome your hopes. Get to know them; do things that accommodate them in your life. Take your hopes out, attend to them, polish them, and make them bright."

Yes, I thought, *hope has largely disappeared from my life. I guess that's why I considered suicide, because I had no hope left, and life seemed empty and meaningless.*

Someone interrupted with a question that once again gave voice to my own inner thoughts: "But what if you don't have any hopes?"

"Oh," replied the pastor, "we all have hopes. It may be that you've not been encouraging them. Your hopes may have been forgotten and neglected in your mind; they may have wilted and died through lack of attention. Perhaps some bad experiences with hopes have made you hesitate to welcome them anymore into your life. It may be that those disappointing experiences and negative events have caused you to shut the door of your life to the bright and positive presence of hope. But you don't have to let this happen. Hope often dies of starvation. If it's not fed, nourished, or cared for, it can be overwhelmed by fear and negativity. But I tell you hope is very hard to kill. I'm sure you have hopes, but they may be weak, sick, or lost through lack at attention. I would encourage you, if you've lost hope, to still open the door and give hope some attention and trust. You can begin to entertain your hopes again, and they will revive and bring brightness, purpose, and excitement with them. The decision belongs to you whether you'll entertain your hopes or keep them shut out."

As I listened to the pastor I felt a strange stirring in my own heart. *This is what I really want. This is vital to my welfare and my fulfillment. I've buried all of my hopes and dreams; they're lost. They're absent in my life. Can they be found again? Can I resurrect them? Can I welcome them again in my heart? Are good things still ahead for me?* While I knew the pastor was not talking directly to me, it seemed that what he was saying was exactly meant for me.

"The saddest music we hear from humanity," he continued, "is the sad music of broken dreams and dashed hopes. But even to the most discouraged of us, the wonderful message is that hope can be renewed. We can begin to entertain it again. It can, by deliberate choice on our part, be refreshed and revived."

The pastor looked around the room, keeping eye contact with us, and said, "So please decide that you'll entertain your hopes. Feed them, pursue them, think about them, and believe in them. If they've been forgotten and neglected somewhere in the basement of your life, I want you to bring them out, feed them, nourish them, renew your acquaintance with them, and they'll begin to live again and bring brightness, purpose, excitement, and meaning to your life."

As I listened to this I felt a strange response in my heart. *Could this be true? Had I let my problems suffocate my hopes? Could my hopes be renewed and revived?*

There was a young lady in the group sitting alone in a corner. I noticed her because she was the one person in the group who didn't smile or laugh very much. She was a very serious, perhaps depressed, person with little energy or life. She'd been introduced to me as Jill. I thought that she could be a very attractive girl, but she seemed to neglect herself and didn't take much care of her personal appearance. I was a little surprised when Jill spoke up at this point and asked the very question that was on my mind.

"But Pastor, what do you do when all of your hopes are dead? I think I've tried to entertain hopes, but I've been disappointed so often. My hopes just don't seem to happen. In fact," Jill continued with her head down and not looking at the pastor, "I confess I've been disappointed in hope so often that I'm afraid to believe in it again in case of more disappointment. Does that make sense to you? Can you be afraid to hope in case you're disappointed again? My hopes are gone; they're dead."

The pastor gave some thought to Jill's question and then responded gently but firmly. "No, Jill, they're not dead. They may seem to be dead, but hope can be resurrected."

Jill persisted. "But what if I resurrect them, and I'm disappointed again? It's so discouraging to have high hopes and then have them dashed."

The pastor realized that he was dealing with a very significant problem for Jill. She had apparently lived through some very great disappointments and hadn't learned to handle them successfully. She was in a very discouraged and depressed state. I wondered what the experiences were that had brought Jill to this emotional condition.

The pastor responded carefully. "Jill, let me respond to your question in two ways. First, as you're probably realizing right now, life without hope is a dreary and empty thing. To give up on hope saps all of the life and energy out of living. To believe that nothing worthwhile lies ahead for you, or to think that nothing bright is going to come your way, is a gloomy way to live. To let your hopes die is to be overcome by the negative attitudes towards life—discouragement, fear, emptiness, and depression. To be without hope is to be without purpose. To give up on hope is to accept the opposite and be governed by a negative, dreary, empty purpose-lessness. When you compare the excitement, power, and energy of hope with the dreary depression of hopelessness, you realize that it's much better to live with hope than to live with hopelessness. We must not let our fears hold us back from pursuing our hopes."

I watched Jill carefully as the pastor spoke to her. She nodded in agreement, but the nod was very slow and hesitant and barely discernable. Pastor Lindsey was now talking specifically to Jill. He seemed to forget that the rest of us were there; this was between him and her.

"For a young woman like you, Jill, with all of life before you, and with the gifts and talents that I know you possess, to let your hopes die is a tragedy. I know you've been disappointed in some of your hopes, but when you view your life right now, I think you can see that what you're experiencing is a life without hope—and that is an empty and meaningless affair. Experiencing disappointment in some of your hopes doesn't mean that you should dismiss all hope and give up on everything. The old hopes may be dead, but there are other things to hope for. Bring out new hopes, or refresh the old ones; polish them up and revive them, and once you're hoping again, life will return with some energy, purpose, and excitement."

I could see that Jill was affected by the caring and gentle rebuke of the pastor. Tears came to her eyes and she was unable to respond. The pastor understood her embarrassment, so he quickly picked up his train of thought.

"That's the first thing, Jill—don't give up on hope, because the alternative, hopelessness, is a miserable, life-denying killer. You may continue to exist without hope, but you're dead on the inside. Look again into your heart, and you will find some hopes there. Acknowledge them, entertain them, and they will start to grow and flourish, and life will once again begin to take on some meaning."

His words seemed so appropriate to my own state of heart that I almost joined Jill in letting some tears come to my eyes. I decided that if I got the chance, I'd talk to Jill and find out from her what was behind her great discouragement.

"My second response to your question, Jill," the pastor continued, "is that there is some skill called for in developing right and realistic hopes.

Most often hopes require a great deal of thought and work and skill if they are to be realized. The qualities that give us the skill to pursue the right hopes and see them realized are its two partners—faith and love. Again I say it ... these three qualities work together. Hope without faith and love can indeed bring acute disappointment. You must establish the hopes that are right for you and then know how to pursue them so that they can be realized. This is a journey, a development, and a matter of growth in the Christian way of life."

The pastor now gave his attention to the whole group again. "So, the first point is that hope can be entertained. But this is a choice that you make. You can determine for yourself right now that you will be a person of hope. You can focus on your hopes. You can encourage them and give them the nourishment that strengthens them. You can believe in them. Hope is something that is entertained."

The pastor smiled and looked around at us, giving us opportunity to make comments, but we were all thinking deeply about what had been said and applying it to our present attitude towards the future. My mind was racing. *I've never thought about deliberately entertaining hopes. I thought they just popped up and were there without any effort or purpose on my part, but I can see now that I do have a personal responsibility for developing my hopes and guiding them so that the right kinds of hopes are cultivated.*

When no one spoke, Pastor Lindsey picked up the theme again. "The second element in the definition of hope is a spirit of 'expectation.' It expects good things to happen. It anticipates that great things are still to be accomplished. It's an attitude towards the future. I said in my sermon last Sunday morning that true hope will fill you with anticipation over the future. You stand on tiptoe with excitement and reach forward to the future. Good things are going to happen. Blessings are going to come. New experiences are waiting. New levels have yet to be attained. Hope is a spirit that is exciting. It's an atmosphere of anticipation. A key element in true hope is the spirit of expectation.

"Hope is the spirit of reaching out to grasp something worthwhile that you do not yet possess. It's anticipating that you will reach goals that you have not yet attained. It's expecting great blessings from God that have not yet come. It's looking forward to experiences that you have not yet had. There is in hope an atmosphere of exciting and happy expectation."

One of the ladies spoke up at this point. "But surely, Pastor, there's a difference between Christian hope and wishful thinking."

"I'm glad you brought that up," said the pastor. "Yes, we must differentiate between idle, lazy daydreaming and hope. Wishful thinking is like undisciplined and unrealistic hope. There are many unworthy wishes and desires that arise in the human heart, but we must not equate these wild, unsubstantial, selfish daydreams with hope. Not every wish and desire that arrives in our minds is to be confused with Christian hope. Hope has desires and wishes, but they are disciplined, refined, and channeled. True Christian hope reflects the desires and wishes that God has for your life. They desire to fulfill the purposes for which God made us. Again I remind you that we're talking about a cooperating dynamic trio here. Hope needs the discipline and guidance of faith and love. When your wishes are disciplined by faith and guided by love, your desires become hopes. There are many selfish, sinful, greedy desires that arise in the human heart; there are many wishes that are lazy, wild, unrealistic, and uncommitted. These things must not be confused with Christian hope."

Kyle leaned forward and listened with rapt attention. "So, we're to entertain hope, and hope gives us the spirit of expectancy that what we hope for will become reality."

"Right," said the pastor.

"But not everything we want is necessarily Christian hope."

The pastor nodded his agreement and waited for Kyle to expand on his thought.

"So, how do you know whether something you desire should be cultivated into a hope or dismissed and rejected?"

The pastor nodded "That's a good question, Kyle. There are a number of ways to do that. First, true hope should be built on a solid base; you should have sound reasons for believing it can happen. It's not wild, unsubstantiated dreams. For the Christian, the great foundation for our hopes is the will of God. Does God want this to happen? Does God want me to enjoy this experience? Does God want me to reach this goal? Hope built in the will of God is strong and realistic.

"Second, Christian hope has substance and an element of reality in it. True hope doesn't entail trying to build castles with empty foam and fragile threads; instead, hope means building castles with material that is strong and reliable. Hope is not sitting idly, dreaming that God is going to provide an easy, prosperous, and successful life for us. Hope is not a casual wishing that God would eliminate all of our problems. Hope is built with material that is strong and appropriate. The materials used by hope are our faith, our obedience to God, and our diligence, purposefulness, and effort. Hope draws these materials from our faith and love, hence they are a trio.

"Hope can build when it has faith that what it hopes for is God's will and purpose, and will further the kingdom of God in love. Hope combines with faith and love, so it doesn't encourage a lazy, indolent, attitude to life, but brings a strong, purposeful striving to life. It brings an assurance with it that if I experience the things hoped for, they will be good for me and for others. Hope can see great potential for blessing, but it doesn't encourage the attitude that I can casually and carelessly meander through life and have everything provided for me by a generous and indulgent God. It contains elements that bring purpose and meaning to the lives of everybody. The substance of hope is reality, purposefulness, effort, perseverance, time, and progress.

"Third, Christian hope is clean and refined in its motivation. We want it for good reasons. It fits in with God's will and purpose for our lives. It's not selfish, greedy, or prideful. It will be a blessing to others and fulfill God's calling for us. In fact, as we'll see later on, hope may call for a great deal of sacrifice and work from us, but it's what we want because it's what God wants. True hope issues from a spirit of love for God and for others.

"Fourth, true hope also has a purpose. It has a clear goal and objective. True hopes are not usually vague, but are sharp and well defined. We know and can explain what it is we're hoping for. Hope is more than just an ill-defined wish for blessing and good things to happen. The pictures formed by hope are not hazy and misty, but clear and sharp."

A lady with a puzzled look on her face interrupted. "What do you mean by clear and sharp pictures?

Pastor Lindsey responded. "I've heard Christians pray 'Lord bless us,' which seems to be a general wish for good things to happen. This is nice but rather undefined. What blessings are we talking about? Is it good health? More prosperity? Is it just good feelings, or a good and successful family? Or is it all of these together? The desire for a good life is fine, but it's not quite what we mean by hope. Let me give you a personal example. When I was young, my great hope was to enter the ministry. That's what I wanted, and that's what I believe God wanted for me. If anyone asked me what I wanted to do with my life, I was quite clear that I want to enter the ministry. This is a clearly defined hope. If I hadn't been clear about this, then I might have answered the question with a vague statement of good intentions, such as, 'Oh, I want my life to be a blessing' or, 'I want God to use me.' These are nice, but vague, statements.

Hope is much sharper and clearer than a generalized desire for a good life. My hope was clear; I wanted to go into the ministry. I realized, however, that if my clear hope of entering the ministry was to be realized, there would also be some subsidiary hopes that were connected to it. My hope was going to be built not of dreams, but by reality. If you were to ask me as a teenager what my hopes were, I would have said, 'I hope to go to seminary to train for the ministry.' That was quite clear. I might also have responded, 'I hope to get a job so that I can make some money in order to afford to go to seminary.' These were hopes; they were clear and plain. On the other hand, if you were to ask me as a teenager what my hopes were and I were to shrug my shoulders and say, 'Oh, I just want to be a blessing and live for God and have a good life,' I would be expressing vague, nice feelings, but not hopes."

The lady nodded her head with satisfaction. "Yes, I can see that. Thank you."

Turning back to Kyle the pastor continued. "In response to your question, Kyle, about how we can distinguish genuine hope from vague desires for good things, the fifth thing I'd say is that hope also has an element of commitment in it. You commit yourself to seriously pursuing the objective to which hope points. You commit yourself to doing whatever is in your power to make your hope a reality, and you trust in God for His help and guidance. My hope of going into the ministry involved some clear commitments and sacrifices on my part, mainly years of hard and expensive preparation.

"The sixth thing I would say is that hope is refined. True Christian hope doesn't involve setting selfish, lazy, or greedy goals. Usually the goals are bigger and greater than our own self interest and comfort. I would say to you quite clearly that if you want to live a life of ease and lackadaisical comfort, then entertaining and pursuing hopes is not for you. The great purpose of hope is to stir you up and motivate you to reach out for things you have not yet achieved and do not presently experience. Hope calls for commitment, work, and application."

I could see that Kyle was listening carefully to what the pastor was saying. He was nodding his head in agreement, so I could tell that what was being said was helping him understand.

"Lastly, I would say that true hopes fit your personality. Hopes flow from your heart and reflect the deepest longings and needs of your personality. They are true to what you are and built into the very fabric of your soul. That is why everyone's hopes are different. My hopes are not your hopes. True hopes fit into the kind of person you are and co-ordinate with your gifts and abilities. It's regrettable that many good children have come to grief because they set about trying to fulfill the hopes that their parents had for them, rather than pursuing the deep desires of their own heart. The hopes of the parent don't always fit the character, gifts, or aspirations of the child.

"I believe that God has implanted hopes deep in all of our hearts, and these hopes fit what we are and what we should be doing. Christian hopes are constructed to fit your gifts and personality. Hopes that are quite out of step with the kind of person you are probably aren't true hopes."

"There's no point in someone who is tone deaf and has no interest in music hoping to be a great musician," someone suggested. "Their hopes should follow another direction."

The pastor nodded his head emphatically. "Yes, that's exactly true."

"Also," added one of the ladies, "I think that true hope will inspire you to work. You may dream about being a good pianist, but if you're not prepared to do the work and persevere at the practice the dream demands, then it's not true hope."

"Yes," agreed the pastor. "Hope will push you to work at fulfilling your dreams. You may dream about being a medical doctor, but hope will get you to commit yourself to the years of study and expense that such a dream demands. Hope stirs up passion, desire, longing, and determination in your heart. It expresses the hunger and longing of your soul."

"I imagine," said Kyle, "that many hopes will call for great work, sacrifice, and discipline. If in the light of these costs you decide not to pursue your hopes, then the desire fades away and your hopes begin to die."

"Right," replied the pastor. "And that's why I insist that we see hope as one of a trio. It doesn't stand alone; it stands with faith and love. Faith calls us to work, and love refines our desires. Hope stirs our desires and motivates us to acknowledge the dream and undertake the work and sacrifice necessary to reach the goal we hope for."

Kyle grunted his agreement and sat back on the chesterfield, relaxed and satisfied. I was glad that he seemed satisfied with what the pastor was saying, because it certainly made sense to me. I could see that many of my wild and undisciplined desires were quite contrary to Christian hope. Hope wasn't unfounded optimism, nor was it lazy, inactive day dreaming. I could see that true hope needed to be disciplined, guided, pursued, and evaluated. The pastor implied that this guidance, discipline, and enterprise came from faith and love, but it wasn't clear to me how faith and love fitted that requirement. *I have a lot to learn*, I thought.

"That leads us to the third thing that this definition of hope makes clear," the pastor continued. We know that hope is the expectation of something 'desired.' Hope points to the future. It says, 'I don't have it now, but I believe the time will come when I will have it.' Hope declares, 'I'm not there, but I believe the time will come when I will be there.' The definition would indicate that hope is entertaining an expectation that what is desired will be realized. You're not there yet; it's still to come. It points to the future."

Carol Dexter spoke up. "When you stop to think about it, that only makes sense. If you already possess something, then you don't hope for it. If you have already attained it, then you don't hope to attain it. Hope centres on some things you don't yet have, and it anticipates that they will one day become a reality. Yes, Pastor, I can see that. Hope looks to the future."

"Good," said the pastor. "You can see how this kind of hope will give us purpose and meaning as we look forward to the rest of our lives. We have things we want to attain, experiences we want to happen, and goals we want to reach. It's the pursuing of these deep, heartfelt goals that brings purpose, meaning, and value into our lives. We're not there yet, but our desire to get there is strong enough that we're going to work and apply ourselves so that one day we will be there. There is a great deal of joy and satisfaction in knowing that we're making progress towards our hopes, even though they are not yet fully realized."

"I can see how this applies to life in general," said one of the group members, "but how does it fit in with our spiritual lives?"

"This concept of hope is very rich for our inner spiritual lives," the pastor replied. "We all realize, I think, that in our Christian experience we still have a lot of progress to make. We could all get to know God better and live closer to Him. We don't yet love as we should love, serve as we should serve, or obey as perfectly as we should, but a lively hope keeps these goals in mind and gives us the hunger in our heart that stimulates us to pursue them. The very experience of pursuing them brings joy and reality, because we know we are making progress, even though at the same time we can see we still have much progress to make. Hope gives us a strong desire for a deeper experience with God. We want to know Him better and enjoy His presence in a fuller and more complete way. In our walk with God there's always improvement to be made and growth to take place, which is why Jesus said, '*Blessed are those who hunger and thirst after righteousness, for they will be filled.*'[1]

"It's those who seek that shall find, and to those who knock that the door will be opened. It's to those who ask that it shall be given. Hope for an even greater experience of God inspires us to pour energy into the processes that generate spiritual growth and development.

"While spiritually there's always going to be room for improvement, hope sends us on exciting and satisfying journeys. Although happy with our progress, we always look to the future for even more. In our walk with God, there is always more to learn and greater things to experience. The hymn-writer puts it well when she says:

> *More about Jesus would I know,*
> *More of His grace to others show;*
> *More of His saving fullness see,*
> *More of love who died for me.*[2]

"The energy hope creates in us makes us hunger and thirst to possess more and more of God. While the progress and newness is exciting and fresh, hope tells us there is still more and more to come."

"This helps me," one of the men shared. "I was beginning to think of hope only in terms of my worldly desires. You know, I hope to make more money or achieve a higher position, or there are some things I want to own and possess some day. But now I see that while God is certainly interested in our physical and worldly well-being, and I can hope for these

---

1 Matthew 5:6
2 *More About Jesus*, Eliza E. Hewitt (1887)

things, He's even more interested in what we become and the kind of people we are."

The pastor nodded. "Yes, hope can cover all of life—our careers, our ambitions, our possessions, and our relationships. But it most certainly emphasizes our spiritual desires to be the kind of people God wants us to be."

As I listened to Pastor Lindsey talk about hope and a bright hopeful future that was worth striving for, I realized that I'd drifted into a way of life in which I didn't think in terms of hope. Instead, I thought in terms of defeat, problems, and disappointments. I focused on the past and present and how bad they had been. I wasn't thinking of, or anticipating, the future at all. When I thought of the future, it seemed to be just a continuation of the past and present. It would simply repeat the disappointments, fears, and discouragements of the present. In fact, the future seemed so bleak to me that I'd decided there was nothing there for me but more pain and emptiness. No wonder I'd seriously thought of suicide. I looked around at the rest of the people, and they all seemed to be in deep thought. I realized what was being taught was having an impact on them as well as on me.

The pastor smiled at us. "I think this would be a good place for us to stop and have a coffee break. We'll come back to it after you've refreshed yourselves."

I was glad for the break, as I was anxious to talk to Jill. I wanted to know if she would tell me just what it was that caused her hopes to die. It seemed to me that we might have much in common.

CHAPTER FOUR

THE DEFEATED

I mentioned to Kyle that I'd like to take the opportunity to talk to Jill. He immediately facilitated the whole introduction. Taking me by the elbow and leaving Karen to her own devices, he guided me across the room to where Jill was sitting. He introduced me to Jill, who seemed a little shy and shook my hand rather hesitantly.

"You two sit here and talk," he said, "and I'll go and get us some coffee."

Since Jill seemed so shy, I decided to take the lead in the conversation. Due to the lack of time, I got right to the point.

"I'm very interested in what you said to the pastor. The questions you asked seemed very similar to my own. I find my hopes for life, if they aren't dead, have certainly been badly wounded. You said your hopes were dead. You must have had some terrible disappointments that caused you to think like that. It might help me if you'd explain some of that to me."

Jill lowered her head and didn't look at me. Speaking with an uncertain, quiet voice that I had to strain to hear, she said, "Yes, and I can hardly believe that it's all happened. But you're right ... things happened, and I gave up believing in hope. But you probably don't want to hear about it all."

"Please," I said, "I've gone through some bad experiences too, and I find all this talk about hope is really challenging me. It would help if I could talk to someone who's gone through similar experiences and feels the same way I do about hope."

Jill lifted her head a little. "You're new here aren't you?" she asked diffidently.

"Yes, this is my fist time. I'm a friend of Karen's, and she invited me to come because she thinks I need to hear about hope, faith, and love. I confess it's all new to me. It certainly sounds enticing, and most of those here seem to buy into it. It's good for them, but I don't think the people here have gone through what I've gone through, so I'm not sure just how it all applies to my own life. I thought you might be able to help."

Kyle arrived at this point with the coffee. He passed it to us without saying a word.

"If you had known me two years ago," Jill shared, "you'd hardly think I was the same person. I'd just graduated from high school. I found a temporary job to get some money so that I could go to university. I wanted to study medicine and become a medical doctor. My dream was to go abroad as a missionary and use my medical knowledge and skill to help other people who lived in more limited circumstances. I was excited about this dream, and it seemed a very good way to invest my life. At that time I knew what I wanted to do and where I wanted to go, and I could see the way ahead of me. I believed it was going to happen. I felt it was God's will for me and my real calling in life. You could say I was a person full of hope.

"To add to my happiness, I'd fallen madly in love with a man who seemed to be inspired by the same hopes and dreams as I. He was in his first year at university, and he, too, was a Christian who wanted to use his talents in service abroad as a missionary. Life was so wonderful. It was such a dream. We would study medicine, get married, and go abroad as missionaries spending our lives helping less fortunate people. We talked about it. We dreamed about it. We even prayed together about it. It all seemed wonderful."

Jill stopped talking and dropped her head again.

"Tell me, Jill," I said gently. "What happened?"

"He met someone else at the university. He became involved with her and dropped me. He gave up his plans to be a missionary, and he's now pursuing a different course in life. I was devastated. How could God let this happen? I lost all interest in being a missionary. I never applied to enroll in university, and now I'm stuck in a dead-end job. I have no ambitions. All my dreams and hopes are gone. I'm hurt, disappointed, lost. The pastor tells me I should still have hopes and resurrect them, but I don't seem to have the inner strength to do that. I'm depressed because I see no future. I don't like what I'm doing, but I've no ambition or energy to try to change it. I have no hopes." Jill was close to tears again.

I looked at Kyle, hoping he would pick up the conversation from this point, but he obviously had no intentions of doing that. I didn't know what to say, but I certainly understood what Jill was going through, and I could see what she needed. After a moment's silence I began to speak, and I was surprised how easily the words seemed to come.

"Jill, I don't know who this man is, and I can only imagine what a shock it all must have been to you. But listen, Jill … you still have hopes. You just need to reconstruct them without that man. Yes, you can go to university and study medicine. Yes, you can become a medical doctor and apply to go to the mission field. Do what the pastor has advised and take these hopes out. Polish them up. Entertain them and allow them some room to grow and expand in your heart. You can construct another life of service without that man. You have God and the gifts He has given you. He wants you to do more with them than what you're doing. Let hope begin to grow again, Jill, and it will change your whole outlook."

I was rather startled at myself saying all of this, but I noticed while I was speaking that Kyle was nodding his head in support and agreement.

Jill held her head so low that I couldn't see her face, but I thought she was crying. Kyle, realizing that I had gone as far as I could, said, "I think we should pray together." He reached out and took our hands and we all bowed our heads. Kyle prayed for Jill, that she would again become aware that God had a purpose for her life and that He would help her revive the dreams and goals that had died in her. He prayed that she would live her years happily involved doing the very thing that in her heart she wanted to do.

This prayer touched me, and I know it deeply affected Jill, for she was quietly weeping. Suddenly fear gripped me. *Do they expect me to pray too? Am I supposed to pray here? Oh no, I can't do that.*

Jill relieved my quandary. "Thank you so much," she said. "I'm so glad you both understand. Allison, what you said seems so right; I need to give hope a chance to live again in my heart. I guess it's easy when things go wrong to get so focused on your disappointments that you allow yourself to fall into a spirit of hopelessness." Jill lifted her head for the first time and looked at me. "I don't know what your problems are, Allison, but I can tell you that to settle for hopelessness is a dreadful way to live. When you lose hope, all of the negative attitudes take root in your heart and overpower you. An atmosphere of doubt, fear, anxiety, and depression overshadows you. It's no way to live. I'm going to try to be hopeful again."

Jill's words struck home to me. *I need to practice what I preached to Jill. It all applies to me as well, and I certainly must not settle for a life of hopelessness.*

At this point the pastor called the meeting to order again. Kyle and I stood up to go back to our seats, but I felt good about the conversation with Jill.

CHAPTER FIVE

THE VISION

When everyone was settled, Jim Dexter spoke up.

"You know, Pastor, what you're saying about hope has some similarities to what I hear in seminars about leadership in my work. We're constantly being told that we must have a clear vision in our minds about what we want to accomplish. As manager of the bank, I must be the one who has a clear vision of what that bank should do and how it should operate. I must have in mind what kind of bank I want it to become. We're constantly being told that we must set goals and then strive to accomplish these goals.

"What's true of the bank should also be true in our personal lives. We need to have a clear vision of what we want to accomplish, the atmosphere we want to create, and the person we want to become. We need to set goals in keeping with these visions and then work hard to do the things necessary to achieve these goals. This is the language of leadership that I'm taught in the commercial world, but I can see that it also applies to what you're saying here. Hopes seem very similar to what we're talking about when we talk about having a vision. It's a clear concept of what we want to achieve and what we want to become. The excitement of this vision motivates us to work and strive in order to achieve it. We're constantly being told to look to the future ... to see ahead and know where we want to go and what we want to achieve, and that's what gives meaning and direction to our leadership right now. Am I correct in thinking that there's a similarity between personal vision and hopes?"

"Yes, Jim, I believe the principles are the same. The thing I would add is that in Christian circles, hopes are also tied to faith and love, so the motivations that are stirred up by hope are pure and properly disciplined.

If you look at the great men of God in the Bible and in the history of the Church, you'll find that they were men of vision. They had a clear concept of what God wanted them to do and what they were to become. Guided by that vision, they made their decisions and determined their actions so that the vision given by God would be fulfilled."

Jim was getting excited. "You know, I can see that. I think many of the great men that God used were men of great vision. In fact, God seemed to begin the process in their lives by inserting a vision or a goal. He came to Abraham and promised to make his descendants into a great nation. With that hope in view, Abraham began to make decisions and guide his life. God called Moses by inserting a vision into his mind at the burning bush, where God gave him a vision that he was to go back into Egypt and lead his people out of bondage and into a new land that was flowing with milk and honey. In light of that hope, Moses changed his whole direction in life, but it all started with the insertion of a hope into his mind and heart that he accepted and believed in. It seems that great enterprises for God begin with the awakening of a vision and a hope in the heart of the person, who then accepts the hope and believes in it and begins to live so that the vision can be realized."

The pastor sensed Jim's excitement. "Yes! Can you imagine the thoughts that started to go through the mind of the young shepherd boy David when the prophet Samuel came and anointed him to be king? David was still a very young man, but this event changed the whole direction of his thinking, his aspirations, and his decisions. God inserted a bright hope that changed everything—God wanted him to be king."

Kyle seemed to catch the enthusiastic spirit, for he said rather loudly, "Yes! And I think too of what Jesus was doing when he told the disciples:

Therefore go and make disciples of all nations, baptizing them in the name of the Father and of the Son and of the Holy Spirit, and teaching them to obey everything I have commanded you. And surely I am with you always, to the very end of the age.[3]

"He was inserting a new vision into their minds and painting a new picture of what the future was to become and what it would look like for

---

3 Matthew 28:19–20

them. The fulfilling of that vision captivated the whole of their lives from that point on."

The pastor nodded his agreement, and then looking around at us he said with great conviction in his voice, "I believe that God has inserted in every one of us here tonight a vision, a hope. These hopes are like the voice of God saying, 'This hope defines what I want you to do. This is what I want you to become. This is my dream and desire for you. If you fulfill this, then you will fulfill your purpose in life. You will do what you were meant to do. You will become what you are meant to become.'

"The decisions you make and the guidance you accept will be drawn from this basic vision/hope that God has planted in your life. This is what you are about. This is what you were born to do. This is where your destiny lies. The finger that is placed on the launch button of your destiny is the finger of your hopes. Hope is calling you forward to do things for God. Hope is forming the realizations of what you can become and what you are to do. Accepting and pursuing these hopes will become the great purpose of your life. I say it to you again, don't turn these hopes down. Bring them out, polish them, make them bright and clear, and your life will take on an excitement and purpose that will stay with you. The light of these hopes will give you guidance and direction as you make decisions and choices. They'll energize you to work and to strive in order that you may achieve them. They're vital to your spiritual and emotional health and to the proper handling of your purposes in life. God has inserted in your heart certain hopes and directions. Give them attention."

We all sat quietly absorbing what the pastor had said and applying it to our lives. After a few quiet moments, someone spoke.

"This has been really helpful to me. I never thought hope had much to do with my life here on earth or how I lived it. I thought hope had to do with the life to come. We have hope in heaven and in being with God. We hope that all of the trials of this life will be finished and we'll live happily ever after. We hope for the second coming of Jesus and the final victory of good over evil. I suppose that's part of the Christian hope, but I can see now it's more than that. Hope is more than next world stuff; hope also makes alive what I have to become and achieve in this world and in this life."

"I know," said the pastor, "that very often we think of Christian hope only as something that has to do with heaven and living with God in the life hereafter. That certainly is part of it, but I'm glad that we now see it also as a quality that guides and directs our lives here on earth. However, the hope of future blessedness is also important, and I think we need to talk about it. So far we've thought of hope as a quality that helps us handle our lives today. It's good to have visions and dreams and hopes for our future in this life. To live with this kind of hope gives us purpose, guidance, energy, and enthusiasm about what is to come in our lives. Hope, however, does even more than that. An important element in Christian hope extends beyond the confines of this life and this world. As Christians, we also have the hope of life after death, and the future victory of Christ over sin and sickness.

"The Apostle Paul says, '*If only for this life we have hope in Christ, we are of all people most to be pitied.*'[4] Hope in Christ adds great value to how we live in this world, but it does much more than that— it gives us hope for the life to come."

One of the men across the room from me spoke up. "When you said you'd speak about hope, this is what I thought you'd talk about. We hope to get to Heaven. We hope there's a life after death. We hope Jesus will come again. But that's hope for things that come after this life and far into the future. I thought of hope almost exclusively in terms of a good life after death. I didn't think of hope as a quality that would influence what we are today and how we're to live in this world."

As we waited for the pastor's response to this I thought, *This man is expressing what many people think about hope. It's all in the future. It's about the good life after death. It has to do with vague but nice promises that eventually everything will work out and we'll all be happy ever after.*

Before the pastor could say anything, someone else interjected. "Yes! This hope of wonderful experiences after we die is really like 'pie in the sky, by and by,' but it has very little to do with the struggles I'm having right now in my life."

The pastor addressed this statement directly. "You're correct in saying that a large and wonderful part of Christian hope is the expectations we have for life after death. We anticipate Heaven. We look forward to seeing Jesus. We wait with joy for His second coming. To the Christian, these hopes are strong, and we're excited because we anticipate that good things are ahead. In the book of Revelation, the promise is given that there will be a new Heaven and a new Earth, and at that time of final victory God will

---

4 1 Corinthians 15:19

'Wipe every tear from their eyes. There will be no more death or mourning or crying or pain, for the old order of things has passed away.'[5]

"Great experiences await us. Finally, we're going to be with God. This is a great help when we're struggling with problems right now. We can look forward to a time when all of this will be over and we'll be with God. The Christian has a strong hope that finally sin will be destroyed; Christ will be triumphant. We rejoice because we believe that we're on the winning team and God and holiness are going to triumph over sin and Satan. It's not correct, however, to say that this is hollow 'pie in the sky, by and by' dreaming, or that it can have no influence on our lives right now."

The man tried to dispute this idea. "I can see that it's nice to think like this, but I don't see how this hope of future blessedness can influence what we are and what we do right now."

"Oh," said the pastor, "the person who has a strong and confident hope for the future adds a great deal of good value to his life here on Earth. The confident assurance of future blessedness adds a positive and exciting element to life right now. In fact, I would say that those who believe and hope with the assurance of great blessedness ahead are going to live now with a very different attitude than those who have no such hope."

"How can that be?" asked the argumentative man.

"Jesus himself demonstrated the power of hope and showed us how to use it in a practical way," replied the pastor. In the book of Hebrews, the writer says,

> *... fixing our eyes on Jesus, the pioneer and perfecter of faith. For the joy set before him he endured the cross, scorning its shame, and sat down at the right hand of the throne of God. Consider him who endured such opposition from sinners, so that you will not grow weary and lose heart.*[6]

"Jesus, in the midst of his great suffering and shame, fixed His mind on the joy that was to come when it was all over. The anticipation of this great joy helped give Him strength and courage to face His present suffering. It's amazing the strength and courage that come to us when we believe that good times are going to come, even if our current circumstances are difficult. The promise of hope is that the present weariness is not going

5 Revelation 21:4
6 Hebrews 12:2–3

to last, but that there lies ahead of us times of great joy and blessing. This gives us courage to face our problems here. This is why the apostle Paul tell us to *'be joyful in hope, patient in affliction, faithful in prayer.'*[7] True hope brings a spirit of exciting anticipation, joy, and confidence into our lives that helps us handle with strength whatever trials we face.

"Paul also indicated that his hopes gave him great courage: *'Therefore, since we have such a hope, we are very bold.'*[8] In our struggle with evil, we have this hope that Christ has already won the victory, and we will participate in His victory over evil. The hymn writer said it well when he wrote:

> *This is my Father's world,*
> *O let me ne'er forget*
> *That tho' the wrong seems oft so strong*
> *God is the ruler yet.*
> *This is my Father's world,*
> *The battle is not done:*
> *Jesus, who died, shall be satisfied,*
> *And earth and heav'n be one.*[9]

"I can testify to the truth of this," said one of the women in the group. "Just over two years ago my husband, Jim, and our little boy, Jason, were both killed in an automobile accident. When I heard the news I was devastated. I thought I would die. In my grief I had no idea how I could go on living. The thought that gave me strength to keep going was the hope that Jim and Jason were in a better place and that we would all meet again. I drew great strength from the belief that this life is not the end, and I would see them again. Believe me, it was this hope that gave me strength to keep going."

This woman's heart-felt story really affected me. *She's gone through much worse than I have, but she found strength and help to keep going. Here am I thinking of giving up and even committing suicide, while she had the ability to get on with life and make something out of it. There may be more to this hope thing than I realized.*

---

7 Romans 12:12

8 2 Corinthians 3:12

9 *This is My Father's World*, Maltbie D. Babcock (1901)

"I remember the dreadful experience that June went through," the pastor said, "but her strength and grace in the midst of it all was a benediction to us."

There was a pause in the proceedings as we all let the meaning of this sink into our hearts. Quietly the pastor continued. "So the hope of Heaven brings strength, joy, excitement, and anticipation into our lives right now. But the Apostle John said even more. He said this future hope can affect the kind of people we are and the quality of ethical life that we live. Speaking about the second coming of Christ he said:

Dear friends, now we are children of God, and what we will be has not yet been made known. But we know that when Christ appears, we shall be like him, for we shall see him as he is. All who have this hope in him purify themselves, just as he is pure.[10]

"When you're full of hope about the richness of the life to come, you don't want to do anything that will spoil or rob you of your future joy and glory. You want to be ready so that you're in a condition to truly appreciate and enjoy the coming blessedness. You want to be prepared, so you're careful about how you live here and now. You seek to live a life of obedience, love, and grace; a life that'll please Him; a life you'll not be ashamed of when you meet Him.

"Hope is a powerful and significant influence in our lives today. It gives us strength to persevere and fills us with a positive and exciting joy as we anticipate the great things that are to come. My prayer for you is the prayer that Paul had for his Christian brothers and sisters when he said, '*May the God of hope fill you with all joy and peace as you trust in him, so that you may overflow with hope by the power of the Holy Spirit.*'[11]

"True Christian hope brings strength, joy, excitement, and reward to our spirits right now. We don't have to wait until we get to Heaven; the blessing of hope is for now."

There was quietness after this statement by the pastor. I carefully considered his words. *Overflowing with hope? I'm a long way from overflowing with hope. In fact, I seem to be empty of all hope, both for my future in this life and for the life to come. Hope has died out in me.* Along with this realization I also felt

10 1John 3:2–3
11 Romans 15:13

a great longing. I wanted to be a person of hope. I wanted to drink some of the joy, anticipation, and courage that come from the stream of hope. But could all of this really be true? How could I believe and hope for this? I finally got up the courage to speak.

CHAPTER SIX

THE VICTORY

S ince I was new to the group, I felt nervous and awkward at my first attempt to participate. "How do you know all of this is true?" I asked. "It's good to think of Heaven, the joy of the afterlife, and the second coming of Jesus Christ, but how do you know it's real? How do you know it's true? It might not happen. It may all be wishful thinking. It may be we're just projecting our own wishes and wants into the life to come because it suits us to think like that."

As soon as I finished I felt a little uncomfortable, as this was a rather aggressive way to state my thoughts. The pastor, however, didn't seem to object.

"That's why we said that wishful thinking and hope were two different things," he answered quietly. "Hope does have a base and plausible causes for its existence. We do have reasonable grounds for our expectations. They're not simply figments of our imagination or fantasies concocted in our own mind to help us feel good."

"Well, what is the base upon which we can have hope?" I asked.

"First," said Pastor Lindsey, "we can have confidence in our hopes because they're the constant assurance given to us in the Bible, the Word of God. They're promises made to us by God through the Bible. We accept the Bible as the Word of God, and the constant message of the Bible is that God has promised eternal life to those who believe in him.

"Second, we have reason to believe because Jesus himself said it. Because so many of the other things Jesus said have turned out to be true, we have confidence that His promises here will also turn out to be true.

"Third, we have a basis to believe these things because of the power and influence they have in our lives right now. They make us better, stronger, more confident people. So you see, our hopes are grounded on a solid base; they're not wishful thinking. They have purpose, they have reason, and they have support!"

I could see the points the pastor was making and wanted time to think about them. Meanwhile, one of the men in the group spoke up, changing the direction of the conversation. "I remember at high school my science teacher used to say that 'nature hated a vacuum.' When there's a vacuum, then something will always try to rush in to fill the empty space. I think this applies to what you're saying, Pastor. If the human heart is empty, something will try to rush in and fill the vacuum."

"Right," replied the pastor. "When our hearts are empty of hope, what are some of the things you think might rush in to fill the space? Hope does have some enemies that are constantly trying to destroy it. What do you think some of the enemies of hope might be?" He waited for us to answer.

Kyle spoke up. "Worry would certainly be one of the enemies of hope. If hope is the happy anticipation that good things are going to happen, then worry is the dreadful expectation that bad things are going to happen."

"Good," said the pastor. "Jesus made it very clear that we should work at building an attitude of hope in our lives and not allow an attitude of worry to dominate our thinking. He said:

Therefore I tell you, do not worry about your life, what you will eat or drink; or about your body, what you will wear. Is not life more than food and the body more than clothes?[12]

"Jesus said that we're to fill our minds with the confidence and trust of hope by seeking '*first his kingdom and his righteousness, and all these things will be given to you as well.*'[13] The building of a hopeful attitude brings pleasant anticipation, while adopting a worrisome attitude brings a cloud of foreboding. You said it well, Kyle, when you said that hope is the happy anticipation of good things to come, while worry is the dreadful expectation of bad things to come. It's better to live by hope."

"I also think that doubt is an enemy of hope," Karen said. "Once you start to have doubts about your hopes, life begins to run out of purpose and meaning. Doubt generates worry and fear."

---

12 Matthew 6:25
13 Matthew 6:33

"I can attest to that," said Jill, who seemed to have a little more life about her. "I know from experience that once you begin to doubt and let it get a hold of you, all your dreams and ambitions begin to collapse. If hope has an element of expectation in it, then so does doubt, but it's an expectation of failure and depression. Once you settle for doubt, you cease to expect good things and only expect bad things. It's hope that keeps you alive. Doubt will kill you."

"These are good thoughts," said the pastor. "What are some of the other enemies of hope that you can think of?"

"I think that apathy or laziness is an enemy of hope," ventured one person.

The pastor thought about that and then said, "You're probably right, but explain why you think that."

"Well," she said, "I think hope energizes you. It calls on you to reach out and stretch yourself in order to attain what you have not yet attained. But to reach your goals and fulfill your dreams will probably demand a great deal of work and discipline. If you're not prepared to work at it, then your hopes will not be realized. So apathy and laziness are also the enemies of hope."

We could all see this, and the pastor nodded his agreement.

The group seemed to be on a roll now, for someone else quickly added their thought. "I think fear is an enemy of hope. Hope inspires you to try, to reach, and to climb. Fear, on the other hand, discourages you from any action. Fear of failure is negative and robs you of the desire to try, to risk, and to venture. Fear says 'you'll get into trouble if you pursue that. It'll never happen. You're sure to fail. It can't be done.' When this kind of attitude takes root in your heart, you become afraid to try anything."

The pastor laughed. "You know, we're talking about hope, faith, and love being a dynamic trio in that they pour a positive, inspiring, God-given dream into your life. But the opposite of this dynamic trio is the destructive trio of worry, doubt, and fear. They make us afraid to do anything. They discourage us from reaching out to try anything that's challenging and difficult. They discourage action and kill energy."

The pastor paused here and waited until he was sure he had our complete attention, and then continued emphatically. "It's strange, but people often claim that hope is an impractical thing, but actually the impractical attitudes come not from hope, but from worry, doubt, and fear. They're the things that discourage us from trying. More worthwhile human enterprises have been abandoned because of worry and fear than anything else. They destroy initiative. They kill ambition. They settle for the mundane. People who are dominated by worry, fear, and doubt, will probably achieve very little in their lives compared to what they could have done had they entertained hope, faith, and love. Hope is positive, practical, and exciting."

"It seems to me that hope leads us to a positive way of life," someone added, "and a positive way of thinking, whereas worry and fear and doubt lead us into a negative, self-destructive way of thinking."

"Yes," said the pastor, "hope and faith and love are very positive, happy, exciting qualities that need to be developed in our lives. But it all starts with hope."

At this point Pastor Lindsey laid aside his notes, pointed at all of us, and said with quiet conviction, "I believe God has implanted in each one of you some hopes. These hopes fit your personality and your abilities. I'm sure these hopes have tried to express themselves to you in the past, but it may be that you've not given them much attention. You may even have dismissed them as impossible, or out of the question, or not worth the effort. They're there in the depth of your heart, but they're lying neglected and unused. I want to encourage you now to bring your hopes out. Give them attention. Take them seriously. Don't dismiss them, for hope has to be entertained. You need to give it time and attention. Take it out. Look at it. Define it carefully. Don't be vague or indefinite. Think about it. Pray about it. Talk about it to a trustworthy friend. Accept it and buy into it. Turn your hope into a vision and an objective. Let your hopes begin to excite you and stir you to action. Let the energy of hope begin to motivate you to newer and greater things. Present your hopes to God. Lay them before Him. If you get the encouragement of the Holy Spirit, you'll be assured that these hopes are of God and that they express your real purpose in life and flow out of your basic personality. To live in hope is a wonderful thing.

"I'd like us to spend a few private minutes in quiet prayer. I'd like you to think about your hopes. What would you really like to do? What would you really like to accomplish? What longing lies deep in your heart that needs you to give it a voice? What kind of person would you really like to be so that you can truly respect yourself? Never mind what others might think at the moment ... this is between you and God. Try to state it clearly: 'My greatest hope for the rest of my life is ... I have a deep desire to ... More than anything else I would like to...' Don't worry about whether you think it's possible or not. Don't consider at this moment how it can be done. If it's true to your heart, it will discipline itself and sharpen itself as it unfolds. The issue right now is to determine your hopes—how you'll go about realizing them is for another day. These deep-seated hungers of your heart and soul are the base for your hopes, but they may need you to take them out, admit their existence, and give them credence and credibility."

Although silence reigned in the group, the atmosphere became intense as we all bowed our heads in heavy thought. I was not used to this kind of internal examination. I'd never before tried to define or outline my hopes, but I knew I had to try. *I know I want to finish university—I can start there. Why do I want to finish university? What do I want to be? What do I really want to spend the rest of my life doing? What do I want in life more than anything else? What would I feel satisfied with if I achieved it? And what about my spiritual life? Do I want to get involved with God? Do I really have a hunger for fellowship with Him? Do I hope He'll become an important part of my life? The pastor said my predominant hope should be to get to know Christ. Am I really interested in that?* As I thought on these things I realized I had more questions than answers, but I knew that I would need to pursue this, and that if hope was to be meaningful to me, I'd need to work my way through these questions. It wasn't going to be easy.

After a few minutes the pastor called for our attention again. "We're talking about hope. Hope is very important because that's where the process starts, but hope doesn't stand alone. Just hoping for something isn't going to make it happen. Just hoping doesn't cause it to appear in the real world. Hope standing alone doesn't accomplish much. That's why hope must be joined with faith and love. Hope could be compared to the architect of a building project.

"We're glad to have Allison here tonight," he continued, looking over at me. "I haven't had a chance to talk to her, but Jim told me that your father, Allison, is a very competent and effective architect."

I nodded my agreement, wondering where this train of thought was leading.

"So consider Allison's father. He's been given the responsibility of designing the new conference centre downtown. His job is to dream and envisage. He has to see in his mind's eye the kind of suitable building that must go up there. He goes to his office each day to work on this conference centre. He sees it in his mind. He puts the design on paper. He has a clear picture of the building in his creative imagination. It becomes an absorbing task for him to understand just what this building will be like. But he is the architect ... he doesn't build the building.

"In his mind he may see the whole thing in its beauty, usefulness, and design. But if you go downtown to the site where it's to be built, all you'll find is empty lots. There's nothing there. The dreams of the architect do not build the building. The function of the architect is not to build the building, but to envisage it. If the building is to be built, then the plans and dreams of the architect must be handed over to the construction engineer, who takes the plans of the architect and begins to build the building. The concepts created by the architect in his mind and put onto paper are now transformed into real bricks, two by fours, and concrete. The architect performs a vital function—the building will be built according to his design—but he doesn't build the building. Hope is like the architect. It forms the dreams and creates the vision of what we want to build and experience in our lives. To develop these hopes is very important, but if all we do is hope, the dreams will never be fulfilled.

Hoping is the quality that designs what you'd like to achieve, but it doesn't take on the responsibility of achieving it. Our hopes will never be realized if all we do is hope. Just as the concepts and visions of the architect have to be turned over to the construction engineer if the building is ever to be built, so our hopes have to be handed over to the department of faith, and faith will take the dreams and vision of hope and turn them into a real fulfillment. Hope and faith work together. Hope is the architect that dreams and creates the appropriate visions. Faith takes those visions and turns them into reality. Next week when we meet we'll talk about faith."

With that the pastor concluded his remarks and passed the meeting back to Jim Dexter.

Jim expressed, on behalf of the group, how much we appreciated the pastor coming. It had been a helpful and insightful time for all of us. He then reminded us that refreshments were available and told us to relax and enjoy each other's company for a while.

CHAPTER SEVEN

THE FATHER

As the meeting began to break up, Kyle, who was still sitting between Karen and me, turned to me and with a friendly smile said, "It was great to have you come tonight, Allison. I've enjoyed meeting you. I hope you'll come again."

"It's been a very interesting experience for me," I replied. "In fact, it was also rather challenging, but I think I needed the challenge."

"Great! Since we're all going to university," he said, looking at Karen and me, "why don't we meet one day for lunch?"

"That's a good idea," Karen answered. "Why don't we meet on Thursday at noon in the cafeteria?"

Obviously pleased with this arrangement, Kyle said his goodbyes and left. Karen and I helped ourselves to more coffee and stayed around to talk with some of the people for a while. I also had a chance to talk again to Jill, whose spirits seemed to be reviving.

"You're looking better already," I said.

"Oh, I think I'm beginning to understand that all is not lost and I can still have hopes. I'll need to revive them and encourage them, or 'entertain them' as the pastor says, but already I feel the cloud lifting and some sunshine beginning to break through."

"I'm glad for you," I said.

"What about you, Allison? Did the discussion on hope help you?"

This question challenged me. "It was certainly interesting," I answered slowly, "and gave me a lot to think about. But I don't think I'm quite ready to start on a new journey yet."

Jill reached out and took me by the hand. "I'll pray for you, Allison," she said earnestly. "Perhaps you and I can journey out of depression and towards hope together."

I was moved by her sincerity. "Thank you, Jill. We'll keep in touch."

I couldn't promise to pray for her, since I didn't know how to do that, nor could I commit myself to the spiritual journey from depression into hope at this time.

After some pleasant conversation, Karen and I excused ourselves from the group, which seemed to be settling in for a lengthy and warm time of fellowship. Jim and Carol Dexter accompanied us to the door. As we were leaving, Jim turned to me.

"It's been really good to have you tonight, Allison," he said. "I hope you'll come again next week."

We thanked them for their hospitality and walked out to Karen's car. As we drove home, Karen asked the inevitable question: "Well, how did you like it?"

"It was interesting," I said. "It certainly introduced me to a lot of different ideas and thoughts. It's also very new to me. It's made me think in ways that I've never thought before. I certainly liked the people; they were very friendly and down to earth."

"But is it going to help you put your life back together?" Karen persisted.

"I can't say yet, but I can certainly see how creating hope in my own mind and heart could open up a new attitude towards life. You're going to have to give me time to think about this."

"Certainly," said Karen, "but do think about it. I know that deep down you must have hopes that fit your character and are appropriate for your life. Find them. Examine them. Entertain them."

Yes, Karen, I'm going to do that.

I was anxious to get to the quietness of my own bedroom and have time to think over what I'd experienced that night, but when I got home my father was in the kitchen making some coffee. He was anxious to talk.

"So, where have you been tonight?" he asked by way of opening the conversation.

I hesitated, not knowing how my father would react to my being at a Bible study. There seemed to be no way out, so I told him.

"My friend Karen has been attending a Bible study group and she invited me to go with her tonight."

My father, spooning the coffee grinds into the percolator, stopped in mid-motion and turned to me.

"A Bible study," he said in a surprised tone. "That's different."

"Karen has become a good friend, and she thought it might help me."

"What kind of Bible study was it?"

"We met in someone's family room. There were about twenty of us. They're mostly younger people, not too much older than I am."

"What did you talk about?"

It was beginning to feel like a cross-examination, and I was becoming uncomfortable and defensive.

"Tonight they talked about hope, and it really was very interesting and challenging."

"Hope," said my father. "You mean we're all going to go to Heaven when we die and live happily ever after?"

"Well, there's a lot more to it than that."

My father was still holding the spoonful of coffee grinds, obviously expecting me to expand on that statement. I didn't feel competent to get into a discussion on hope with my father, who was clearly a little suspicious of this new venture in my life.

"Father, they are very nice and ordinary people. They're not religious weirdoes or narrow-minded fanatics. They're ordinary, nice people who are exploring the spiritual way of life. The pastor was there to talk to us about hope. It was all very friendly and nice."

My father put the coffee into the percolator.

"Besides," I continued, "the meeting was in the home of Jim Dexter, the bank manager. I think you know him."

"Jim Dexter," repeated my father with surprised recognition. "Yes, I know Jim. He's a good, solid man. If he's there, then I feel a little more relaxed about it."

"The pastor led the meeting tonight," I explained, "but I understand that normally it's Jim himself who leads it."

"Does it meet every week?"

"Yes,"

"Are you going to go next week?

"Yes, I think I will."

My father still seemed hesitant. "I wish I'd more information about this group. I don't want you getting all mixed up with some weird religious crowd. You're still in a very delicate emotional state"

"I can assure you they're not a weird religious crowd," I laughed. "Talk to Jim Dexter if you want, or to the pastor himself. They'll be able to explain the purpose of the group much better than I can."

I was anxious to get to my room and have a little solitude, so I said good night and left my father to his coffee and his questions.

It was with gratitude that I closed my bedroom door and sat down to do some serious thinking in the friendly silence of my own room. As I thought, some things became evident. First, I hadn't done a very good job of my life up until this point; I was discouraged, disappointed, and depressed with myself. I knew I was built for something better than what I'd become.

Second, I had no desire to continue on the same track that I'd been following. I needed to change and pursue a different type of life.

Third, I understood from the Bible study that I should have deep within me some fundamental hopes that come out of my basic personality, and that I need to let these hopes emerge and construct my life around pursuing them. These hopes will express my destiny and purpose, and will give meaning and satisfaction to my life. I sensed these hopes were there, but I didn't know what they were. I felt I was on the verge of a great discovery, but what the discovery was I still had no idea. I felt a mixture of excitement and fear—excitement because I sensed that some great insight was within me and wanted to emerge, and fear because I knew that if I did allow this insight to emerge, it would call for changes and differences in me that would transform my whole life. Did I want this? Should I pursue this, or close the door on it all before it really came to life within me? What should I hope for? What was my purpose in life? What should I set as my goals and objectives? Somehow I understood that the answer was within me and only needed recognition and it would burst upon me. Once it did, I would never be the same again.

I'd never been one to pray much, but now, in the quietness of my bedroom and in the midst of the turmoil in my heart, I thought I should try. Feeling rather strange about the whole thing, I knelt by the side of my bed—because I thought that was the thing to do—and ventured to pray.

O God, I'm not very good at this, and I'm sorry that I haven't prayed to You very much before. Help me now. I feel that great changes are taking place in my life, but I don't know what they are. I feel a whole new way of life is emerging, but I don't know its shape or its nature. I want my life to go in a different direction, but I don't know what that direction is. Please help me and guide me. I want to know what my purpose is in life. I want to know what my basic hopes should be so that I can spend my life pursuing them. I want to hope for the right things. I want to be excited and full of anticipation again. Please help me to get this right. Please help me not to make mistakes. Amen.

Although this kind of praying was new to me, I felt more at rest once I'd finished. I understood that I'd made a basic decision in my heart that I was going to seek and pursue a different way of life. It wasn't at all clear what that would be, or what I should expect, but I knew I had started on a journey—an important inner journey. It was as if I could now hear a different voice calling to me, and I'd made a commitment to try to hear that voice and follow it. I went to bed and slept soundly all night ... a very unusual occurrence for me.

CHAPTER EIGHT

THE DIRECTION

I found myself pleasantly looking forward to the luncheon with Karen and Kyle. In fact, I had to admit to myself, Kyle was often in my thoughts. His pleasant, friendly face kept presenting itself to my mind—unbidden, but certainly not unwelcome. When Thursday came and Karen and I entered the university cafeteria and saw Kyle sitting at a table waiting for us, I noted the pleasure I felt at seeing him again. Kyle greeted us with his usual friendly, energetic smile, and we were soon engaged in happy conversation.

After a few minutes of casual talk, Kyle changed the direction of our talk. "I've been thinking a lot about the session on Tuesday night. I've gone over in my mind what was said about hope and keep asking myself about my own basic hopes. I guess I hope for a lot of things, but I'm trying to pass over all of the trivial and unimportant hopes to get down to the very basic things. What do I really want to do with my life? If I had one thing I really wanted to achieve, what would it be? What do I want to invest my life in more than anything else?"

"I've been thinking about the same thing," I said, glad that Kyle had brought the subject up. "I think there are many things we can hope for that are trivial and incidental, and that's alright. But in addition to this, I sense that there are also, deep within us, very basic hopes that are fundamental to our personalities. We're built to fulfill these hopes. They express our destiny and calling. I've been thinking along the same lines as you, Kyle. What would I like to do with my life more than anything else?"

"Right," said Kyle. "If I had a vision of what I'd like to accomplish in life, what would it be? I guess we have to try to zero in on one or two very fundamental issues. What am I on this earth to do and to accomplish? If I had only one thing to hope for, what would it be?"

"I thought you said you were studying to be an engineer," I said. "Isn't that what you want to do with your life?"

"Yes," said Kyle, "I'm certainly interested in that, and I'll continue to study for it, but when I think about it, I don't feel really passionate about it. I think you need to feel really passionate about the fundamental hopes of your heart."

I continued to press him, because this idea of being passionate about your hopes seemed right to me. "What do you feel really passionate about, Kyle?"

Kyle looked at me thoughtfully for a while before answering. "Do you know what I feel really passionate about? When I think about it, I get excited and stimulated. My heart seems to leap within me."

"No, tell us what it is."

Kyle hesitated. I could see that he wanted to tell us, but was reluctant because he wasn't sure how we'd react.

"Well," he finally ventured, "it may sound a little farfetched, but I'd like to become an engineer. If I become qualified as an engineer, do you know what I'd really like to do with it?"

We waited.

"Well, you know," Kyle continued uncertainly, "I've been around a lot of church buildings in my life. I look at them, and some of them are very nice and fit the functions they're supposed to fulfill, but many others seem quite out of joint. They're not constructed well, and they're not appropriate for the service they're trying to fulfill. Some are downright ugly and unappealing. Some are cheap and in disrepair; they don't present a good image. Some are growing churches and have had pieces added to the building that look all out of harmony. You know what I'd really love to do?" In his excitement Kyle had forgotten to be shy and backward about this. "I'd like to become a qualified engineer, and then make my services available to churches to help them build suitable buildings, or extend and renovate their present buildings. I'd like to help churches with their buildings, so that they expedite the ministries that the church would like to accomplish. There's such a need there, and churches don't always know how to go about it. They need guidance and they need help, and many of them don't have a lot of money. It would be a joy for me to help struggling and growing churches with their buildings and facilities so that they could use them to get on with the work of God more effectively."

I looked at Kyle and saw that his eyes were sparkling. His face was alive; his body language exuded excitement. He was expressing his heart and defining his deep desire. It was his hope, and it certainly wasn't far-fetched or unrealistic. It fitted his skills and his personality, and his whole heart was in it. This was his passion.

I leaned forward, and with more enthusiasm than I'd felt about anything for a long time, I said, "Then do it, Kyle. I know you can do it. It sounds wonderful."

Kyle seemed relieved that we accepted his dream and his hope without being critical or doubtful. I realized this was a very important issue for Kyle, but also in its freshness it was very delicate and we could have easily crushed it with a negative reaction. He was clearly pleased at our response and thanked us for our encouragement.

"What about you, Allison?" Kyle asked. "What's your hope for your life? What's your passion? What do you want more than anything else?"

I wasn't quite ready for that question and didn't know how to react.

"To tell you the truth, Kyle, I don't really know. I'm studying optometry and it's interesting, but I don't feel any passion about it. It would be a good job, and it's something that I feel I'm capable of doing. Looking after people's eyes is important, but when you talk about passion and excitement ... no, I don't feel passionate or excited about it."

"You think your heart lies in some other direction?" Kyle asked.

"Yes, I think my heart lies somewhere else, but please don't ask me what it is. I don't know at the moment. I just think there's something else out there that I should hope for that would satisfy me and excite me much more. But I don't know what it is."

"Well, don't give up on it, Allison. That's the message of hope. Discover your hopes and dreams, and then take them out and polish them up until they're bright and clear. They'll excite you and motivate you, and you'll be passionate about them. Then life will be exiting and full of anticipation. Isn't that what hope is all about?"

Kyle and I had almost forgotten about Karen, who sat quietly listening to us and observing us.

"What about you, Karen?" I asked. "What are your hopes? What are you passionate about?"

Karen seemed to be quite assured and confident. "My thinking seems to be going in a different direction than you two. You're thinking of great things—life's calling, grand accomplishments—and that's good for you, but my heart is set on some things that seem much more mundane and simple. Do you know what I'd really like and what I feel most passionate about? I want to be a mother and have a good home. I want to devote myself to my home, husband, and children. I'll still seek my job in optometry, but that's not my passion. I just want to love and care for a family and devote myself to them. That may sound rather mundane and lacking in ambition to you two, but that's what I really want."

My heart went out to this new friend of mine. What a beautiful person she was.

"Oh Karen," I cried, "I love it, and it seems so right for you. Of course it's not mundane; it's probably the most important job in this world."

Karen appreciated my enthusiasm. "But there's more," she said. "I do have a sense of ministry that would extend beyond my own home and family. My experience of being single and pregnant was traumatic for me. It was a dreadful time. I was lost, confused, and didn't know where to turn or what to do. I longed for someone to talk to and help me, but there was no one. I was afraid, ashamed, and lonely. I made all of the decisions myself, but I desperately wanted someone who understood the situation to advise me and guide me. So my heart goes out to all young women caught in the same circumstances. I want to help them. I've heard of an organization in town called The Pregnancy Centre. Its purpose is to help girls who have become pregnant. They need someone to confide in. Someone to support them and understand them. They certainly need help to understand all of the implications of abortion, and the other alternatives available to them. I want to be part of that organization, and I want to open my home as a place of sanctuary and refuge— a safe place where these girls can go."

I reached over and took Karen by the hand. "Of course, Karen, there's such a need, and I know you could help those girls in crises. I think it's wonderful."

Kyle also seemed enthused, and added his support by nodding his approval of Karen's thoughts. "Yes, it sounds just right for you, Karen," he said.

Karen wasn't finished yet. "Also, when I think of being a hopeful person and letting hope be a ruling quality in my life, I don't just think of the great big issues of life such as my career or life's purpose and objectives.

These are obviously important, but I also think of developing a hopeful attitude in a multitude of little things that we face every day. To think hopefully can become an attitude of mind and a way of living that applies not only to the great issues of life, but also to the many minor events we encounter every day."

Karen looked at Kyle. "Kyle, you called these small hopes trivial and unimportant. I don't think I like them being called that, because behind all of these small hopes is an attitude of mind and heart. A hopeful person develops a hopeful viewpoint about everything. When it's raining, I hope the sun will shine tomorrow. When I think like that, then today's rain doesn't seem so depressing. When I'm getting weary of cold winter, I'm hopeful that spring will soon be here, and winter becomes much more bearable. When someone hurts me, I look for and expect to encounter others who will help and encourage me, and that helps me deal with the hurts. When I'm disappointed over something or someone, I can always hope that tomorrow there will be an improvement. Hope causes me to look for this and anticipate it. When I'm weak, I can hope in God that He will help me, for He is strong. When I fail, I can hope that I'll do better the next time.

"Hopefulness is a state of mind and heart, so it enters every part of life—important and unimportant—and it brings strength, anticipation, happiness, and brightness to all of life. I want to live with hope. I want to be a person of hope. I want hope to influence every part of my living. I want all of my attitudes to be ones of hope, and I think that will help me become the person I want to be and to live the life that I want to live. I think it'll help others as well and encourage them in the midst of their disappointments and difficulties. Hope is an attitude towards all of the events and people in our lives. It becomes a way of thinking and a way of dealing with hardships and setbacks. I know from experience that to lose hope is a dreadful thing. Hope is powerful, bright, and exciting. As the pastor says, it's dynamic. Real hope is precious to us and brings great value and meaning to our lives."

This was a long speech for Karen who was usually quite quiet. I was amazed at the depth of her understanding. I realized that she'd come through great disappointments and hurts, and that she had not arrived at this hopeful attitude easily or naturally. She had to deliberately cultivate this spirit in spite of the prevailing adverse conditions in her life. I felt my respect and confidence for her grow within me. *Here's a person who's come to terms with life and decided that it's going to be good and not bad, worthwhile and not useless. She knows how to deal with life in a bright and confident way.* I also realized that I was far from being the hopeful person she was describing, and I began to feel the desire to be like her and to enjoy the same hopeful feelings.

Kyle obviously felt the same way. "You're right, Karen. We need to develop a sense of hope for all of life, not just the big issues. We need to cultivate hope every day and in every situation. Hope is broad in its scope. We need hope to develop the right objectives and purposes in life, but we also need hope to keep the atmosphere bright in the small, every day, mundane matters of life. Hope is not a big savings account we only draw upon for an emergency or a large purchase, but it's a credit card that covers all the daily expenses of life."

"Right," said Karen. "We don't lock it up in some safety deposit box and forget about it until something major occurs. We keep it in our purses and wallets to be available for constant use."

We all sat silently thinking about this for a while until Karen spoke again. "There's something else I think about hope."

I looked at her as my appreciation for her depth and strength continued to grow.

"We tend to think of hope primarily in the external world," she continued. "We hope for things, achievements, purposes, and objectives that we wish to possess or attain, and that's good and certainly a part of it. But I think hope should also be applied internally. You asked me what I felt passionate about, and I told you that I want to find a loving husband, have a warm home in which to raise a family, and have a ministry that will help girls in distress. That's what I hope for very deeply, but all of that is external to me—it's outside of me. Internally I also have some very passionate and overwhelming hopes. There's a kind of person I want to be. I hope for and passionately long for a closer walk with God. I want to be the kind of person God would be pleased with. I want to be the kind of person that I can respect and enjoy being. I have inner longings that are very strong that I hope will be fulfilled and satisfied. My hopes extend not only to what I want to possess, achieve, or devote my life to, but also to the kind of person I want to be. I hope to become a godly person and a person of love who's Christ-like in spirit. I hope to develop a faith that can keep me victorious in all the trials of life. I hope to live close to God and get to know Him. I have spiritual aspirations that keep me reaching and stretching for a closer fellowship with God."

In all of my contacts with Karen she'd never revealed herself to me as she was now. I realized that she was a thirsty spirit and a hungry soul, and I felt I understood her better than ever before. What I saw now I liked, respected, and in many ways wanted to emulate.

Kyle was the one who responded to Karen. "Oh, Karen! You've really hit the nail on the head. Of course you're right—our hopes should not only cover the success and achievements of our external life, but also extend into our hearts and the kinds of people we want to become. We can have confidence that God will help us become the people we should be. Cleanness of heart and authenticity in spirit is what He favours and desires for us. I think this is what Jesus was talking about when He said, *'Blessed are those who hunger and thirst for righteousness, for they will be filled.'*[14] These inner longings for righteousness are good, and the promise is that they shall be filled. God will help us."

Karen nodded her agreement. "I thought a lot about the passage the pastor quoted from Paul's letter to the Philippians:

I want to know Christ and the power of his resurrection and the fellowship of sharing in his sufferings, becoming like him in his death, and so, somehow, to attain to the resurrection from the dead.[15]

"Paul' great spiritual hope was to get to know Christ better and better. I have such a hope."

"I know that verse," said Kyle, "and I think there's more to it than even that." Kyle reached into his pocket and took out a small New Testament. He opened it, found what he was looking for, and began to read.

But whatever was to my profit I now consider loss for the sake of Christ. What is more, I consider everything a loss compared to the surpassing greatness of knowing Christ Jesus my Lord, for whose sake I have lost all things. I consider them rubbish, that I may gain Christ and be found in him, not having a righteousness of my own that comes from the law, but

---

14 Matthew 5:6
15 Philippians 3:10–11

that which is through faith in Christ—the righteousness that comes from God and is by faith.[16]

"That's what I hope for," said Karen with intensity. "I want to know Him better and please Him. I want His spirit to be in my heart. I want to be clean and holy; I want to be a person of love and joy and hope. When you talk about hope, that's what I hope for more than anything else."

"Wonderful," said Kyle, "and that's a hope that has substance and provision, for God will help and God will guide in the pursuit of that hope. Didn't He promise to help us become good and holy people?" He turned to another verse in the Bible and read.

May God himself, the God of peace, sanctify you through and through. May your whole spirit, soul and body be kept blameless at the coming of our Lord Jesus Christ. The one who calls you is faithful and he will do it. [17]

"This is a hope that certainly can be realized and fulfilled, for God has promised to help us through Jesus Christ."

The conversation now was between Kyle and Karen. All of this quoting the Bible was a new world to me, but I did sense the spiritual hopes that they were expressing and knew that they were correct. The conversation awakened something in me that longed for what they were talking about.

"So," said Karen, looking at us, "we all have hopes. Let's take them out. Entertain them, polish them up, and pursue them, for the pursing of our hopes is the right direction in life."

I felt I had to agree with her, but my hopes had become so uncertain and faint that they would need considerable encouragement if they were to be revived and renewed. Even though the way seemed difficult and new to me, I knew it was far better to be a person of hope than to continue to live in the hopeless state I'd been in. I felt I was making progress, and I felt thankful to Karen for introducing me to this whole matter of hope. I could no longer dismiss it easily and carelessly as vague, wishful thinking and "pie in the sky by and by."

The rest of the lunch went well, and as we were parting Kyle suggested that we do it again, to which both Karen and I agreed.

---

16 Philippians 3:7–10
17 1 Thessalonians 5:23–24

"Good," said Kyle. "I'll see you both at the Bible study on Tuesday night."

I was rather surprised to find myself looking forward with anticipation to the next Bible study. When I returned home later that day I found my father waiting for me. He seemed to have something he wanted to say, so I lingered around the sitting room until he brought the subject up. Finally he said, "I talked to Jim Dexter today."

I was immediately alert.

"He mentioned that you were at his Bible study last Tuesday."

I nodded but stayed silent, knowing there was more to come.

"He explained it all to me, and I feel a little more comfortable about it. I certainly have confidence in a man like Jim."

Still I waited.

"I explained to him that I was uncomfortable about you getting into a religious group, especially since I had no idea what kind of group it was. He assured me that it was quite orthodox and not extreme in any way."

Again I nodded, but didn't say anything.

"He said that he was having lunch with the pastor of the group this coming Tuesday and he thought it would be good if I joined them."

I felt a stab of alarm go through me.

"He said it would give me a chance to meet their leader and ask some questions, so I've decided to do that."

"What!" I cried. "The pastor doesn't know anything about me. I don't want you telling him about the abortion and the attempted suicides. He knows nothing about all of that."

My father raised his hands to calm me down. "I promise you I'll say nothing about any of that. If he gets to know it'll be because you told him. I only want to meet him, see what kind of person he is, and make some inquiries about the church. I'm interested in the group and would like to know what they're about."

I knew my father well enough to know that I couldn't change his mind, but I felt uncomfortable with him inserting himself into this new part of my life. So feeling rather upset and uncomfortable about the arrangement he'd made with the pastor and Jim Dexter, I retired to my room.

SECTION II

Faith: The Construction Engineer

CHAPTER NINE

THE WORK

O n the following Tuesday, my father phoned to say that he would be working late that evening, so I never got a report from him about how his luncheon went with Jim Dexter and Pastor Lindsey. When Karen picked me up to go to the Bible study, I was feeling rather anxious about what happened at that meeting. Jim welcomed us at the door and made no mention of it. The pastor, however, came over to me as soon as I arrived.

"Allison, I'm glad you were able to come tonight. I had the privilege of meeting your father today. Jim and I had a very enjoyable lunch with him."

I tried to appear relaxed and smiled. "Yes, he told me that he was meeting with you, but he had to work late so I never heard from him how the meeting went."

The pastor assured me that he found my father a very good and interesting person. "We talked mostly about the new conference centre project that he's working on right now. It was fascinating to hear all the details about it."

I was relieved to know that I hadn't been the main topic of conversation, and I sensed from the open, relaxed way the pastor was talking that he hadn't received any vital or sensitive information about me.

"In fact," the pastor continued, "if you don't mind, I'd like to use your father as an illustration of what we're going to talk about tonight. What he's doing with the conference centre is a good way to show the connection between hope and faith."

I had no idea how my father could be considered a good illustration on the connection between hope and faith, so I laughed and said, "I'll be interested to hear about that connection myself."

We all settled down with Kyle, once again, sitting between Karen and me. Jim Dexter opened in prayer and then turned the meeting over to the pastor.

I was rather surprised that as the pastor was preparing to begin his talk, Jill spoke up and asked for the privilege of sharing with us her experience of the past week. The pastor of course was very willing for her to go ahead and do this.

"I want to tell you all how much last week's session on hope helped me."

I looked at Jill and realized that she was indeed quite different this week from the discouraged and despondent person she'd been the week before. Even her appearance and grooming had improved. She spoke with her head up and with some sense of confidence. Clearly an inner change had taken place.

"I was so disappointed and discouraged with what had happened in my life that I'd given up. I'd lost all sense of hope and purpose. I'd sunk into a state of despondency where I accepted defeat and was convinced that it wasn't worth my while to attempt doing anything significant with my life. I felt I'd no future and had nothing to live for, and I didn't have much hope that things would change."

I listened, fascinated with the transformation I could see in Jill. Jill turned and looked at Kyle and me.

"Last week during our meeting, Allison and Kyle came over to talk to me. The conversation helped me very much. In fact, it jolted me enough that I awakened to the fact that I did indeed have hopes and I needed to revive them and renew them. I was so grateful to them for their gentle understanding and care."

I was surprised at this praise, thinking we'd not said anything of great significance to Jill, but I also noted a flow of happiness come over me at the thought that I'd been able to help someone else in their struggles.

"With the encouragement of the meeting last week," continued Jill, "I went home and decided to bring up my hopes again and to nurture them, try to believe in them, commit myself to them, and start to pray about them." Jill looked around at us with a little confident smile on her face. "It's hard to put into words just what a difference that change in attitude makes."

"Why?" someone asked. "What's changed?"

"That's just it," responded Jill. "When you look at the outside of my life, all of the externals are just the same. I'm still stuck in a dead-end job. I've not gone to university. I'm still deeply grieved in my love life. Being a missionary doctor seems a long way off. Externally nothing has changed, but internally things are very different. I'm beginning to dream again. I'm beginning to believe I can emerge out of this negative depression and once again see the possibilities of a life of service. While nothing has changed externally yet, I believe that if I listen to my hopes and believe in them, I'll start making decisions and adopting attitudes that will change the externals of my life. I feel like once again I have a purpose, and I want to find out what that is. I'm excited and anxious to get started on it."

The group responded to this with spontaneous applause. Jill's eyes filled with tears, but this time there was a smile on her face as she nodded to the group, expressing her appreciation for the support. I felt pleased that I had a small part in this transformation.

The pastor smiled at Jill. "Thank you, Jill. That's encouraging for all of us. I can assure you that things will begin to change as you entertain your hopes and begin to pursue them. The change has started already on the inside in your own heart and spirit, and it won't be long before you make decisions and pursue new directions that will bring significant changes to your external life. But it all begins in the unseen attitudes of the heart. It starts with hopes— entertaining them and believing in them. Jill, I want you to know that we all believe in you and support you, and we'll help you any way we can as you begin your new journey." Many in the group nodded their encouragement. "In fact," Pastor Lindsey said, "why don't we take time right now and pray for Jill. Let's pray that God will lead and guide her as she pursues her hopes for the future."

I was rather moved as I listened to the prayers that were said for Jill. They seemed so genuine and encouraging. *These people really care and are getting behind Jill. They're such a support.* Jill obviously felt the same thing, for she wept quite openly as the people prayed for her.

When the prayers were finished, the pastor was ready to move on with the Bible study.

"Last week we talked about hope, which we defined as 'entertaining the expectation of something desired.' We said that the hope-filled person has a much better attitude when dealing with the future than the hopeless person. Also, the hopeful person presently experiences a brightness and excitement about life that the hopeless person doesn't have. The hope filled life has stronger elements of expectation, excitement, and brightness than the hopeless life. Hope gives us joy and strength for living this life and fills us with confidence about the life to come.

Last week I encouraged all of you to entertain your hopes, welcome them, and develop them. Please excuse the repetition, but it's very important for you to understand that hope doesn't stand alone. Hope by itself doesn't achieve or accomplish anything. It gives guidance, inspiration, and motivation to help us pursue our objectives, but by itself it doesn't achieve them.

You may remember that I likened hope to an architect, who dreams and envisages the building. He's the one who designs it. The building begins in the mind of the architect, but he doesn't build it. If the building is to be built, the visions of the architect have to be passed on to the construction engineer. He takes the dreams and designs of the architect and translates them into an actual building that we can see and feel and live in. When an architect and builder cooperate, the building moves from being a good idea in the mind of the architect to an actual structure, built with bricks, two by fours, and concrete. Hope, if you like, is the architect, and faith is the construction engineer."

The pastor paused here and looked at me. "I had the privilege of having lunch today with Allison's father. He's the architect who's designing the new city conference centre that has been in the news so much lately. We had lunch at a restaurant close to where the centre is to be built. I looked over at the proposed site. There's nothing there. It's an empty lot. In fact, it looks quit neglected. It's full of weeds and rubble, and some people have dumped trash on it. As I looked at this untidy, vacant space and listened to Allison's father describe the large, impressive building that's going to be built there, I had a hard time connecting the two. The building was clearly established in the mind of Allison's father. He could describe it, tell how large it would be, how high it would rise, how deep the foundations needed to be. He told about the material it would be built with, and the uses to which it would be put. He could even tell me where the entrance would be and how many rooms there are. He knew about the design of the windows and the heating system. It's going to be a marvelous and awesome structure that will be the pride of our city. But right at the moment, if you go down to the site and have a look, there's nothing there; it's all in the mind of the architect. The physical building doesn't exist, and it will never be built unless those plans are given to the construction engineer. The building will never happen as long as it stays only in the mind of the architect. A lot of work, skill, expenses, and patience will be necessary if the dreams of the architect are to become a reality.

"Hope is like the architect. It dreams and envisions what we want to do and the kind of person we wish to become. The clearer and sharper the visions, the more power and inspiration they'll give. But you must never imagine that hoping for something will, by itself, make it happen. The dreams and inspirations of hope must be passed on to the next department, and that is the department of faith. It's the job of faith to take the visions of hope and work at them and turn them into reality."

The pastor picked up his Bible. "If you have your Bible with you, I'd like you to look up a very important verse, Hebrews eleven, verse one. In this chapter the writer is describing faith and the wonderful things accomplished by people of faith. In the first verse of that chapter he defines what he means by faith. He says, '*Now faith is the substance of things hoped for, the evidence of things not seen.*'[18] Faith takes the dreams and visions of hope and gives them substance. Faith takes the unseen inspirations of hope and brings them into the real world so that they become evident. It's the job of faith to take the visions of hope and turn them from aspirations into reality. Faith is the quality that takes the dreams of hope and does what's necessary to make the dreams come true. It takes the spiritual longings of hope and translates them into visible, experiential realities. The evidence that hope and faith are working together in our hearts is seen when our hopes begin to turn into reality. Faith gives substance to our hopes and makes reality out of inner aspirations. When that conference centre begins to be built and we see it beginning to take shape, that will give evidence and substance to what, up to this point, has been an unseen dream in the mind of the architect. The unseen dream begins to take shape as construction starts. Hope is given substance. The unseen begins to show evidence of reality. Faith takes the hopes of the heart and works at making them real and giving them outward evidence. Faith takes the dreams of hope and causes them to happen."

As the pastor used this illustration of my father, I could see clearly the connection between hope and faith. I'd never thought of such a connection before. I was pleased he used my father as a good illustration, but I wasn't sure that my father would've been pleased.

"Another significant verse is found in the book of James," continued the pastor. "James makes it clear that true faith manifests itself in action. If you truly believe something, then you'll do something about it. He states that quite clearly. *'In the same way, faith by itself, if it is not accompanied by action, is dead.'*[19] In verse twenty-six of the same chapter he says, *'As the body without the spirit is dead, so faith without deeds is dead.'*

The power and essence of faith is that we do something about what we believe in. So hope and faith work together. Your hopes are empty daydreams if you don't trust them enough to start doing something to make them a reality. Hope without faith is just wishful thinking. Faith without hope could be a lot of empty activity without real purpose or direction."

I looked around the group, and it seemed that everyone was deep in thought. What the pastor was saying made good sense to me, and I think others in the group were trying to absorb the implications of his teachings. No one spoke, so the pastor continued.

"Another important verse is 1 Thessalonians one, verse three: *'Remembering without ceasing your work of faith, and labor of love, and patience of hope in our Lord Jesus Christ, in the sight of God and our Father.'*[20]

"The dynamic trio—hope, faith, and love—are tied together again in this verse, but it's important to note how Paul introduces each of them. There is the *patience* of hope, the *work* of faith, and the *labor* of love. The descriptive words before each of these qualities are important. What hope needs more than anything else is *patience*. We have dreams and hopes, and we wish we could realize them right away. We don't want to wait; we long for them and want them now. When you have a strong hope and it stimulates you, gets you excited, and inspires you, then you want to possess it and experience it right away. But sometimes the things we hope for are a long way off and will take time, patience, and perseverance if they're ever to become a reality. Sometimes between the dawning of a bright hope and its actual realization there is a long period of time. Most often when we hope for something worthwhile we don't get it the next day, there is usually a great process that takes place before the hope becomes a reality. It's this process that makes us impatient. We become impatient with the delays,

19 James 2:17
20 KJV

discouragements, and detours that we must experience before the hope become a reality. So hope needs patience.

"But notice the antecedent of faith is *work*. If you really have faith in your hopes and believe in them, you must be prepared for a great deal of work, discipline, and commitment. Faith is the quality that puts together a realistic plan on how to make our hopes a reality. Faith recognizes the difficulties that lie between the dawning of a hope and the realization of its actual reality. There are difficulties and problems blocking the way, and faith sets to work and finds solutions to them. Faith works at overcoming the roadblocks and discouragements. Faith can end up calling for a whole lot of hard work and strenuous effort. The 'work of faith' often demands significant perseverance and discipline if many of our hopes are to be realized.

"Jesus gave an illustration of this when he talked about a man who decided to build a tower. He said:

Suppose one of you wants to build a tower. Will he not first sit down and estimate the cost to see if he has enough money to complete it? For if he lays the foundation and is not able to finish it, everyone who sees it will ridicule him, saying, 'This fellow began to build and was not able to finish.'[21]

"You want to build a tower—that's the hope, that's the dream, that's the objective. There's nothing wrong with that dream, but Jesus said it's only sensible to sit down and count the cost and make plans. Where will I build it? What shall I build it with? How long will it take? How much is it going to cost? Do I have enough resources to actually build this thing? To turn the hope of building a tower into the real thing becomes the work of faith."

The pastor paused to let the significance of this sink into our hearts. We were all very quiet. One lady spoke rather quietly.

"This is different from what I thought. It seems to me that if you believe in your hopes and have faith that they can be realized, it may turn into a whole lot of hard work."

"You're correct," said the pastor. "In fact, you can see that if you want to primarily look after your own ease and comfort, if you want to live an undisturbed and unchallenged life, then hope, faith, and love are not for you. They're a dynamic trio. They'll disturb you, motivate you to action, and cause you to step out into new areas and perhaps take some risks.

---

21 Luke 14:28–30

They don't point to an easy, slothful life; instead, they challenge and stimulate us to action. Laziness, fear, and self-indulgence are not comfortable in the presence of hope and faith. Faith often calls for a whole lot of hard work, effort, and risk. But it's also a life of adventure, excitement, fulfillment, and satisfaction."

The pastor paused and someone spoke up. It was the same young man who'd been a little aggressive in his questions the week before. His name was Edgar. As Edgar spoke, I sensed an edge of anger and disbelief in his voice.

"That's very different from what I perceive faith to be."

"Tell me what you thought of when you thought of faith," responded the pastor.

"Well," said Edgar, "I thought faith meant believing in God. You wanted God to do something for you, and if you had strong enough faith, God would eventually do it. Faith believes that God will act and respond to our prayers by doing what we ask Him to do. Faith is believing that God will do it, so it doesn't involve all of this work, discipline, and human effort on our part."

The pastor, sensing Edgar's resistance, listened carefully to what he said. He paused for a moment or two before responding. "Let's look at one or two illustrations to help us get a correct understanding of just what our part is and what God's part is. I heard a story once, and perhaps you've heard the same story. It's a little farfetched, and probably not true, but it does illustrate what we're talking about.

"There was a fine, wealthy Christian lady who built for herself a very expensive house up on a hillside overlooking a beautiful lake. She had a large window constructed at the front of the house where she could look out and see the lake with the mountains in the background. It was a very beautiful spot. After the house was completed and she'd moved in, she was a little distressed to see a large oak tree down the hill a little that blocked out much of her view. She was a loyal church lady, and she remembered the pastor had preached one Sunday on faith. He quoted Jesus as saying:

... I tell you the truth, if you have faith as small as a mustard seed, you can say to this mountain, 'Move from here to there' and it will move. Nothing will be impossible to you.[22]

---

22 Matthew 17:20–21

"On the basis of that statement the lady prayed very earnestly that night before going to bed that the Lord would move the tree during the night so that in the morning when she got up the tree would no longer be there and she would have a clear, unspoiled view of the lake and the mountains. 'After all,' she thought, 'if God can move a mountain, it's not asking too much for Him to move a tree.' So she prayed and had all of the faith that she could muster and went to bed. With some excitement she got up the next morning and went immediately to her large window, wondering if a miracle had happened overnight. She pulled back the curtains and was somewhat disappointed to see that her view was blocked by the same old tree."

I noted that quite a number of the group smiled at this rather far-fetched story. I wasn't sure if they were smiling at the fantasy of the woman, or because they could easily predict the outcome of her prayers. Edgar, however, didn't smile.

"I think," said the pastor, "that someone needs to sit down with this earnest lady and have a talk with her and ask her what she was really hoping for. The conversation would probably go something like this:

"I hoped that tree would be moved out of there. It's spoiling my view."

"Your objective is to move the tree?'

"Yes."

"Do you believe it's possible for that tree to be moved?'

"Yes, certainly."

"If you believe that the tree can be moved, let's do what Jesus told us to do and sit down and count the cost and figure out how it can be done. Let's put our faith to work. Do you have a wood saw?"

"Yes."

"So we could get rid of the tree by sawing it down?"

"Well, yes, but I'm an old lady and I can hardly do that. Besides, if we did it that way, the dead tree would be lying there and that wouldn't be nice."

"You're fairly well off; money is not a problem for you, so you could hire someone to cut the tree down and cart it away and clean up afterwards."

"Yes, but it would have been easier and cheaper if God did it."

We all laughed at this lady's misplaced faith, but Edgar didn't think it was funny.

The pastor continued. "The lady finally decided to pay workers to come and cut the tree down and take it away. One day she got up and looked out her window, and the tree was gone. Her objective had been realized and her faith had worked its way through the problem. It's true that God could have done it, but He didn't; He expected her involvement. He wanted her to make a contribution.

"Now," smiled the pastor, "a more realistic illustration, if she doesn't mind, is Jill. She dreams of one day becoming a medical missionary doctor. That's a very worthwhile hope and dream, and I've no doubt that God will help Jill do this, if it's His will. But do you think God by his Spirit is going to suddenly fill Jill's mind with all of the medical knowledge she'll need? Is God going to suddenly, without practice or experience, endue Jill with all of the skill and ability of a surgeon? Will God one day bodily lift Jill up and transport her over the oceans to Africa? God could do it. We don't doubt the power or ability of God, but I think He will call on Jill to become involved in the process. She'll have to go to university. She'll have to train as a surgeon. She'll have to equip herself as a missionary. It can be done. It should be done, and God will help her do it, but it will take the cooperation and patience of hope along with the work of faith to make it happen."

"Well," said Edgar in a rather disgruntled voice, "I sometimes think God could do a lot more than what He does. What you describe seems like a lot of human effort. It's all of the flesh and it leaves nothing to the working of the Spirit of God. If God would do more, it would save us a lot of bother, cost, and effort."

The pastor replied rather firmly. "If God is going to do it all, and all we have to do is sit around believing and asking, then God is going to end up with a lot of lazy, indolent, and immature followers. If we have no involvement or responsibility in the work of God and His kingdom, then we'll not grow in grace or mature in character. God wants us involved because the effort and demands of active obedience help us develop in our faith, grow in holiness, and deepen our sense of appreciation and fulfillment when we actually experience what we want. There are real values for us that can be realized only by our personal involvement in the purposes of God."

Edgar was clearly not yet convinced. "It just seems like a lot of trouble for us to go to when it could be much simpler if we could just trust God and let Him do it."

"Simpler? Yes. Better for us? No." The pastor took his Bible and opened it. He clearly didn't agree with Edgar's attitude and was dealing firmly with it. "Jesus often referred to his followers as servants of God. In fact, the apostle Paul went even further, calling himself a slave of Jesus Christ."

Looking at Edgar the pastor asked, "Edgar, what do servants do?"

"They work for their master and serve his needs," Edgar replied reluctantly.

"Exactly. Servants don't sit at home all day thinking that since the master's got lots of money and resources, he can do everything for himself." The pastor now opened his Bible. "Once Jesus was moved by the great needs of the crowds that followed him. Let me read what the Bible says:

But when he saw the multitudes, he was moved with compassion on them, because they fainted, and were scattered abroad, as sheep having no shepherd. Then saith he unto his disciples, The harvest truly is plenteous, but the laborers are few; pray ye therefore the Lord of the harvest, that he will send forth laborers into his harvest.[23]

"Jesus is calling for laborers to go into the harvest field. What were these laborers expected to do, Edgar?"

"I suppose they were expected to work in the harvest field."

"Right! I imagine God could reap the harvest all by Himself without our help, but He doesn't do it that way. He calls for our involvement and work so that together the harvest will be taken care of."

The pastor was not finished yet. He pointed to his Bible again. "The apostle Paul refers to Christians as soldiers who have to put on the whole amour of God and get involved in the battle with evil. *'Therefore put on the full armor of God, so that when the day of evil comes you may be able to stand your ground, and after you have done everything, to stand.'*[24]

"We are soldiers, Edgar. What do soldiers do?"

"They fight in the battles."

"Of course they do. Soldiers don't sit in their tents and say, 'I believe God is big and able enough to fight His own battles. He doesn't want me out there risking life and limb when He could quite simply win the battle for Himself.'

"Paul also told us that the Christian life is like a race and we are the athletes. Athletes must prepare themselves to run the race. They don't

---

23 Matthew 9:36–38 (KJV)
24 Ephesians 6:13

compete by sitting at home saying 'if God wants me to win the race, He's capable of preparing me to do it.' Athletes successfully run by training and preparing themselves."

The pastor looked around the room to be sure we were all listening. "Now Edgar has raised a very important point about how faith operates. You get the picture from the words *servants, slaves, labourers, soldiers,* and *athletes.* They are "doing" words. They are "involving" words. They don't give the impression that all we have to do is have faith and God will do the rest. It's false to think that we can sit at ease at home and trust God to do all that is necessary. A faith that doesn't include action and deeds on our part is leading us in a false way. Remember the words of Jesus: '*Not everyone who says to me "Lord, Lord," shall enter the kingdom of heaven, but only he who does the will of my Father who is in heaven.*'[25] You get the picture from these words that we are involved in doing God's will.

"God expects us to work with Him; to cooperate in His work and to be used in furthering His kingdom. God will certainly be with us and help us and empower us, but we must do our part. God will do what we cannot do, but it pleases God to use human personality to express and do His will. God has a part to play, but we also have a part to play. God wants to use us, not displace us. So again I say it—faith is the quality that believes our hopes can be realized and is prepared to go about doing what is necessary to realize them. Hopes that don't issue in faith are useless daydreams. The level of your faith is determined by what you're prepared to do about your hopes. Believing that God will fulfill all of our hopes while we sit idly by trying to have faith will be very disillusioning.

One of the other men spoke up at this point. "I agree with what you're saying. If an athlete wants to compete but lacks faith in his ability, he won't go to the effort of training. If a soldier is convinced he'll lose the battle, he'll try to avoid the fight. Faith has to believe in our hopes enough for us to work at realizing them. If you're sure they'll never happen, you'll lose heart and won't work at it."

"Right," said the pastor. "Faith and hope work together. They don't do well on their own. They're a duet. If you don't want to do anything about your hopes, then your faith is weak."

I agreed with the pastor and could see his point. It's necessary for our growth and well being to be personally involved and cooperative in what

---

25 Matthew 7:21

God is doing. I had no difficulty with that, but I could tell that Edgar was feeling rather rebuked. As I looked at him I sensed that his questioning and argumentative attitude were really a screen for his inner problems of faith. I wished I could help him, but I knew I was too much of a novice in these spiritual matters to be of much help.

Others now joined in the discussion. One asked, "But Pastor, I thought that when God saved us and granted His salvation, we received it from God by faith and not from things that we have done?"

"Yes," replied the pastor, "that's correct. We're saved by faith. I think of what Paul said to the Ephesian church:

> *For it is by grace you have been saved, through faith—and this not from yourselves, it is the gift of God—not by works, so that no one can boast. For we are God's workmanship, created in Christ Jesus to do good works, which God prepared in advance for us to do.*[26]

"Some things are quite beyond our power. No matter how hard we try, we cannot do them. Some things, if they are to happen, will need the presence and power of God in our lives; no amount of human endeavor will accomplish them. We can never by our own efforts or good deeds find favour with God. Our redemption in Christ comes to us as the gift of God by faith, but even in the faith that brings salvation to us we are not entirely uninvolved or passive. It's true that we're forgiven and brought into fellowship with God by trusting in His grace and love to provide this for us, but God expects us to be involved in the redemption process. We are still asked to repent. This salvation results in a changed life and changed behavior. The verse says that although we receive the salvation by faith and it's not of ourselves, it does, nevertheless, issue in action. We're expected to do the good works that He's designed for us to do.

Faith issues in obedience. Trust expresses itself in humble commitment to His will. Hope and faith create a spirit of cooperation between God and us. God can do some things that we cannot do. God will not do some things that we should do for ourselves. Faith for salvation results in changed lives, new hearts, and a new allegiance to a new Master and Lord who wants us to adopt new values and priorities. Faith results in a changed

---

26 Ephesians 2:8–10

way of life. If there is no change in the way of life, then one has to question the authenticity of the faith."

This was heavy stuff. It was stretching my mind to understand it, but from what I could grasp, it all made sense to me.

Edgar still seemed to be a little on edge. "What about miracles? We can't perform miracles, but Jesus seemed to say that if we wanted miracles to happen, we would need to have faith."

"That's a good question," responded Pastor Lindsey, "and I think we should give it good consideration. Why don't we take our coffee break right now and then we'll talk about faith and miracles when we come back."

CHAPTER TEN

THE OPPOSITION

During the break, I was rather surprised when Edgar immediately made his way over to the chesterfield where we were sitting and asked if he could talk with us. I was glad that he took this initiative, as I felt that he had some problems that lay behind his questions, and that he needed to deal with these problems and give them attention. I could sense a deep inner struggle going on in his heart. Edgar was about my age and seemed to be a rather tense individual. He was serious in his approach to life and very earnest. I could tell that the conversation with him was not going to be humorous or flippant.

"I just don't seem to get this faith business at all," began Edgar. "I thought that having faith meant that we were to trust God, and He would do all kinds of things for us. Just have faith, and God will provide. Have faith, and God will act. Have faith, and God will do miracles. I've been trying to have faith, but nothing seems to happen. It just doesn't work the way I think it should."

I didn't feel that I was an expert on faith, but I sensed that Edgar had problems and was looking for help, so I ventured a response.

"The pastor seemed to be saying that faith is largely a doing word. If we trust, God will help certain things to happen, but we have our part to play. When you try to have faith, Edgar, do you do anything yourself to help make it happen?"

"But that's the problem," said Edgar. "I think I would just get in the way. My efforts would mess things up. I feel I have to just stand back, let go, and let God do it His way."

"I think you're right, Edgar. But doesn't doing it God's way mean letting Him work through us and involve us in the solution?" I looked at Kyle and Karen for support. "I think that God's way often involves using people to do His will."

"But that seems so much of human effort. It's as if it's all up to me, and God has nothing to do with it at all."

"Not at all," I said. I was surprised at my forthrightness. "God expects us to exercise our spiritual muscles and strengthen our spiritual fiber, and that won't happen if we sit idly by trying to have faith and leaving obedience, personal commitment, and discipline out of the equation."

I wondered why I was doing all of the talking while Karen and Kyle sat watching, but I seemed to be possessed by a conviction that Edgar had some inner problems that were beginning to reveal themselves. I continued talking.

"I think, Edgar, that you want all of your hopes to be fulfilled without great effort on your part. You hope for God to do great things, but you don't want to take any risks, assume any responsibility, or be burdened with the personal discipline necessary to help God make it happen. I don't know much about all of this, but I don't think God gives us hopes and faith so that we can live an easy, lackadaisical life. Your kind of faith, Edgar, seems to encourage spiritual laziness. It places all of the responsibility on God and denies the importance of obedience and commitment on our part."

I was startled at my bluntness. I looked again at Kyle and Karen for support. I had carried the conversation out to a point where I didn't know how to get back. I could see from the look on Karen's face that she, too, was surprised at my speech, but she rallied to my support.

"Yes, that's right. Suppose I hoped to go on to university after high school, but didn't have the money to do it. What should I do to turn my hope of a university education into a reality? I could sit at home and pray and try to trust God to provide the money. I could meet the postman at the door every morning to see if God had sent an unexpected check to me in the mail. Or I could go out, look for a job, and earn some money to cover my university expenses."

"Do you hear what she's saying?" I said to Edgar. "Is one way spiritual and the other fleshly? Or do hope and faith work together to make God's will happen?"

Kyle now joined in the discussion. "I feel like God wants me to become an engineer, but in order to gain my certificate, I need to achieve high marks. Since I think this is God's will, what should I do when exam time comes? Should I neglect my studies in order to pray a lot, and pray that God will help me with the exams?"

"Of course not," I interjected again, "I'm very new to this, but I suspect, Edgar, your ideas about faith would encourage us to develop a spiritual indolence and pander to a harmful spiritual laziness."

I could see that Edgar was rather taken aback by the bluntness of my statement. Feeling rather amazed at my boldness, I looked at Karen and could see that she thought I was being too blunt. Kyle had a little incredulous smile on his face. I felt my face go a little red and understood that I had crossed over the line of acceptability. I was glad when the pastor rescued me from my embarrassment by calling the meeting together again.

While Edgar made his way back to his seat without responding to my comments, Karen whispered to me, "Allison, where did all that come from?"

"I don't know," I said, still feeling embarrassed. "It just came over me that Edgar needed some kind of jolt to shake him out of his wrong way of thinking. Do you think I should apologize to him after the meeting?"

Kyle jumped into the conversation at this point. "What would you apologize for? Saying something that he probably needed to hear very badly? I think if he listens to you he'll receive a great deal of help."

"I certainly hope so," I said rather humbly. But I was still uncomfortable at speaking so forthrightly to Edgar, especially since I was still new to the group and the subject.

CHAPTER ELEVEN

THE COST

hen we were all settled again, the pastor continued his talk. "As
I listened to your conversations over the coffee break, I gath-
ered that some of you are concerned that the way I've presented
hope and faith make them look like a very human endeavour that can be
done without much reference to God. You think from what I've said that
it would be easy to see hope as simply human envisioning, and faith can
be understood as merely a matter of positive thinking and human effort.
Where does God come into all of this? Then Edgar asked about miracles,
which are clearly the action of God and beyond the possibilities of human
endeavour. So let's talk about this, because hope and faith are important
Christian virtues. They play an important role in the living out of the Christian experience and are vital for the quality of our fellowship with God, so
we must understand them well and comprehend just how they operate."

The pastor reached into his pocket and drew out a set of keys. Holding
them up, he continued. "What I have here is a set of keys. They're all keys;
there's nothing here that's not a key. Although they're all keys, they all perform different functions. The purpose of a key is to open something that
would otherwise be closed to me. One of these keys is made to start my car.
Another one will open the door of my house. A third one is the key to my
office at the church. They are all keys; they are essential for giving me access
to vital parts of my life. Without them, I would be excluded from essential
things. While they're all keys, each key plays a different role. The key to my
car doesn't help me get into my house. My office key won't start my car."

The pastor put the key ring back in his pocket. "In the same way, there
are different aspects to faith. Faith is a spiritual key that opens up great

spiritual possibilities that otherwise would be closed to us, but faith operates in a number of different ways. For example, there is the faith we have in our creeds and in our beliefs. We believe in the Apostles' Creed. In fact, the Apostles' Creed begins with the words, 'I believe,' and then lists the things we believe. That's one aspect of faith. Then there's the faith we have in the moral and ethical standards that are expected of believers. In the book of Acts, we're told that the early believers were *obedient to the faith.*[27] They were changing their lives to conform to the expected standards of the Christian lifestyle. That's another aspect of faith. Then there is saving faith. This is the faith we have in the love, power, and willingness of God to forgive our sins in response to our trust and repentance. They are all faith, but faith operates in different ways.

When it comes to the type of faith that works with hope and love, we could call this particular aspect of faith achieving faith. Achieving faith is the belief that what we hope for can be experienced and achieved. Achieving faith is the faith that God will give what He's promised to give and will do what He's promised to do. If your hopes are inspired by God and in the will of God, you can have simple faith that God will give all of the help and direction necessary for these hopes to be achieved. But be sure of this—there is a definite divine presence, endorsement, and activity here. If it were all of the flesh, if we were left to ourselves and God was absent, then a number of things would happen.

First, we'd probably start to wish for and hope for different things— things outside of God's will. Selfishness would creep in. Secondly, we wouldn't have the inner stamina or strength to pursue things that were God's will. We'd probably settle for the easier, self-indulgent desires of our heart. Left to ourselves, much of the life that encompasses God's will and purpose would be lost. Without God, we are powerless to do His will and would rather live a self-centred life.

"Now listen carefully," said the pastor. "I believe in miracles. I believe in God's presence and involvement in our lives, but miracles happen mostly to those who are obediently following the will and purposes of God for their lives. If you look at the scriptures, you'll see that miracles mainly happen to those who are obediently following the hopes and dreams God has given to them. Miracles don't happen much to those who are sitting

---

27 Acts 6:7

idly at home wishing for great things to come their way. Miracles happen to those who are out there pursuing the purposes of God for their lives."

The pastor sat back and relaxed a little. No one said anything. We were all waiting on him to expand on what he meant. "There's an interesting story in the life of Abraham. When Abraham was old and was looking for a suitable wife for his son Isaac, he didn't want him to marry one of the local pagan girls, but wished to find a wife from among his own relatives and people. So he sent his chief servant on a mission to his brother-in-law's home to look there for a suitable wife for Isaac. The servant asked God for guidance and he received it. Through a number of remarkable events, he found the young woman, Rachael, and brought her back as the prospective wife for Isaac.

"When he was reporting on his journey to Abraham, he said a very important thing. He said '*I being in the way, the Lord led me to the house of my master's brethren.*'[28] He believed God led him because he was 'in the way' —fulfilling his master's wishes and doing the job that had been assigned to him. It was while he was doing all of this that the Lord led him. Now," said the pastor with emphasis, "suppose he was not in the way? Suppose he got side tracked? Suppose he decided to run off and get lost with all of the money and gifts his master had entrusted to him? Would the Lord have led him? Would God's miracles have followed him? Miracles happen, but mainly to those who are in the way, obeying their faith, following their dreams, and pursuing their hopes."

Jim Dexter spoke up at this point. "I'm thinking of Moses. The same principle would hold true in his life. God gave him the wonderful hope that he could lead his Israelite brethren out of the bondage and slavery of Egypt and into a new and prosperous land. So when did all of the miracles begin to happen? The greatest miracles happened when Moses obeyed, went into Egypt, and started the task God had given him. Would the miracles have happened if Moses had rejected God's vision and had gone to hide again in Midian?"

There was a general agreement in the group as a number shook their head in response to Jim's question. The pastor also agreed.

"That's true, Jim. And when did the miracles largely stop? When the Israelites decided not to go ahead with God's plans, but wandered in the wilderness for forty years."

---

28 Genesis on Galatians 24:27 (KJV)

"Of course," said Jim. "And when did the miracles start again? When they decided, under the leadership of Joshua, to obey God and enter the Promised Land. Remember when the children of Israel were going to cross the river Jordan and the waters of the river dried up to make their journey across much easier? But when did the waters of the river dry up? Did it happen when the Israelites sat at the side of the river and waited for God to part the waters before they ventured in? No. They were instructed to carry the Ark of the Covenant into the waters, and when the priests entered the water, the river dried up. That's a great principle, Pastor. Miracles happen largely to those who by faith are obediently pursuing the purposes of God for their lives. They don't happen very often to those who are disregarding the visions that God has planted in their hearts, or aren't prepared to follow them."

Now it was Kyle's turn to add to this conversation. "It's the same in the New Testament. When Jesus sent the disciples out two by two, they were able to perform miracles. If they'd decided not to go but to stay comfortable and safe at home, would the miracles have occurred?"

Pastor Lindsey smiled. "Yes, you're getting the idea. God does wonderful and marvellous things for those who by faith are obeying Him and following His instructions. Remember also the wonderful promise Jesus made to the disciples when he said:

Therefore go and make disciples of all nations, baptizing them in the name of the Father and of the Son and of the Holy Spirit, and teaching them to obey everything I have commanded you. And surely I am with you always, to the very end of the age.[29]

The pastor shook his head a little. "I've heard part of that verse quoted like this: 'Surely I am with you always,' as if it's a blanket promise that Christ's accompanying presence will go with us regardless of where we are or what we're doing, and without reference to our obedience and trust in Him. But that's not what is promised; instead, He promises that as we go about the task of fulfilling His command to make disciples, He will be with us, even to the ends of the world and to the end of the age. Like most of Christ's promises, this promise is conditional on obediently fulfilling the job and purpose that God has for us.

---

29 Matthew 28:19–20

"So," the pastor said with emphasis while looking at Edgar, "we must understand that we can expect God's presence and power when we're going about the business of pursuing with faith the hopes and purposes that God has set in our hearts. You can expect wonderful things to happen as you entertain your God given hopes and do the work of faith to make them happen. People who faithfully pursue the objectives that God has set for them see the mysterious, unexpected, and powerful blessing of God on their lives. We can't expect to see this to any great extent if we neglect our hopes, or fail to do what is necessary to make them a reality. That's why hope and faith are powerful partners in the life of the Christian."

Edgar looked very solemn and thoughtful. The pastor waited to see if he wanted to make any more comments, but he remained silent.

"I say it again," the pastor concluded, "God has placed in your heart some hopes. I want you to entertain them, define them, and be sure they are what God wants for you, and then put faith to work and begin to do all you can to make those hopes a reality. As you go about the business of fulfilling your God given hopes, you can be sure of the supernatural presence, power, and grace of God accompanying you all the way. It's the most exciting and fulfilling way of life. It's not necessarily the easiest way, but it's the best way. Hope and faith, when understood and practiced, are a dynamic duet in our lives. As we exercise them, God's blessing and power ... and, yes, miracles ... can happen in our lives."

There was a quiet acceptance felt in the room. I sensed we all understood the challenge being laid out for us. I certainly felt it in my own heart. I wanted to understand what the hopes of God were for my life. I wanted to know them, entertain them, and then get on with the business of making them happen. This thought thrilled me, and I wondered how I could have lived my life for so long and missed this whole thing. But where would I start? I still wasn't sure what my hopes should be or how to pursue them.

When no one in the group spoke, the pastor picked up his Bible and then stood up. I realized that this gesture was not to announce that the meeting had come to an end, but rather to indicate that what he was about to say had special significance and importance. Once he was sure he had our full attention, he began speaking again.

"God had some hopes and dreams. Way back at the beginning of things in the Garden of Eden, man sinned and broke his fellowship with God. He became corrupt and self absorbed, and was spiritually lost for eternity. But God had a dream. God had a hope. He purposed to provide a way for mankind to be restored into fellowship with Him and live with Him forever. That was a wonderful dream. That was a beautiful hope in the heart of God.

"Then God enlisted faith to the make hope become a reality. God put His faith to work and devised a plan for man's salvation whereby the separation between Him and mankind could be healed. It was a plan to redeem us. It was a plan of faith designed to make the hope become a reality. This path of faith led to a long, hard, discouraging, agonizing journey, but the journey was guided by the hope of ultimately providing salvation for a lost and fallen race.

"It started with Abraham, Isaac, and Jacob. In them God found a few faithful men He could have confidence in and use. Their descendants became the Hebrew people whom God chose and separated. He gave them His law and led them into a land of their own. It took generations to accomplish this, and even then these chosen people disobeyed Him and turned to other gods and rejected His love, but God persevered and continued to pursue His hope."

There was silence in the room. Everyone seemed to be listening with rapt attention. I noticed that Kyle was leaning forward with his elbows on his knees, totally absorbed in what the pastor was saying. I could tell that we all felt that what was being said was vitally important to our understanding of hope and faith.

"He sent prophets to these people," the pastor continued, "to call them back. The prophets were great moral giants of men, spiritually towering above the rest. The prophets were despised, persecuted, and rejected, but God persevered. The journey of faith was long and discouraging, but God had a hope, and faith was working towards its fulfillment.

"Sometimes God had to punish His people. Enemies overcame them and carried them away into captivity, but they learned lessons from this. Progress was being made. God was pursuing His hope; His faith was at work."

I was enthralled with what the pastor was saying. This was all new to me. I'd never heard such things before. I could hardly wait for him to go on.

"Then the climax came. God sent His son, Jesus Christ, into the world in a great exhibition of faith and hope. We all know that it was no happy picnic that Jesus came to. The path of faith led Jesus to Jerusalem. It took

Him into the agony of Gethsemane and led Him through the injustice of Pilate's judgment hall and the shame and mockery of Herod's palace. But God had a hope, and His faith was working at making that hope real—giving it substance and reality.

"But, oh, the cost of faith! It led outside the city walls of Jerusalem and up the hill of Calvary to that great and final battle with physical pain and spiritual opposition. There on the cross Jesus battled with all of the searing, tearing claws of the demons of Hell. As we see Him there, do we know what this is? This is God's faith at work. God had a hope; this is the way His hope could be given substance. This was God's faith at work.

"As we look at this, we can only echo the words of the hymn writer who said:

> *"Man of sorrows" what a name!*
> *For the Son of God who came;*
> *Ruined sinners to reclaim;*
> *Hallelujah! What a Saviour.*
> *Bearing shame and scoffing rude,*
> *In my place condemned He stood;*
> *Sealed by pardon with His blood,*
> *Hallelujah! What a Saviour.*[30]

"But that's how it was. A way had been opened up for us to come back to God. Salvation was now available for a sin-lost race. God's hope had become reality. God's hope had now become substance. His faith had worked out a way, and the great story of redemption was completed in Jesus Christ. But the only way it could be done was for Him to follow the path of faith."

I realized from the intensity and conviction in the pastor's voice that he'd gone beyond just teaching; he was urging acceptance on us. "You have hopes—God given, inspired, and thrilling dreams. They excite you, bless you, and inspire you. If these hopes are to become substance and reality, then their fulfillment needs the combined support of hope and faith.

"Faith is serious business; it's harder work than most Christians realize. That's why God calls His followers "servants" and "labourers" and "co-workers and soldiers in Christ." The call of faith is not for the lazy; it's

---

30 *Hallelujah! What a Saviour!* Philip P. Bliss (1875)

not for those who cherish their ease and comfort. The call of faith is not for the half hearted. The call to faith is a call to work and discipline. It's for anyone who will, in the words of Jesus '*deny himself and take up his cross and follow me.*'[31]

Silence reigned. I glanced at Kyle. His full attention was still focused on the pastor. I looked over at Karen and could see some tears in her eyes. Clearly this presentation had made a deep impact on both of them. The pastor was not finished.

"This is a solemn moment. Destinies are in the balance. You have a dream; you have hopes. I challenge you now—will you believe these hopes? Will you commit yourself to the work of faith to see them become realities? I think we need to spend a little time in quiet and private prayer. As you pray, bring out your hopes. Present them to God. Never mind whether you think they're impossible at the moment or not. That's not the issue. The goal is to discover what hopes God has inserted into your heart. What purposes does God have for your life? Once you accept your hopes, you must believe in them and commit yourself in faith to do all that you can to make them a reality. Then trust God to help you in ways you can't help yourself."

The pastor sat down. Heads bowed. A reverent stillness dominated the atmosphere. Never in my life had I ever experienced this atmosphere in a group of people. A rich solemnity seemed to overpower us all. We were all aware of the deep importance of the moment. We sensed that great spiritual transactions were taking place in that room. Throughout my life I'd participated in many different groups, but never anything like this. I'd been to parties where everyone seemed to be enjoying themselves, but I'd never experienced the depth of communication that I was experiencing now. It was as if God was present and right there with us. I bowed my own head. I sensed that I did have hopes. I felt there was a purpose to my life, but I still didn't know what it was or how I should go about discovering it. I'd started praying in the privacy of my own bedroom, so I prayed now.

Dear God, I sense You have a purpose in my life. I think I have hopes that are buried deep inside of me somewhere. Please help me to find them and discover them. Please help me understand what they are, and then help me commit myself in faith to pursuing them.

---

31 Matthew 16:24

After a period of intense quietness, the pastor concluded the meeting by saying, "Our time together tonight has come to an end. Before we have some coffee and fellowship, however, I'd like to give you this piece of advice. If you're entertaining some hopes and accepting them, but still have some uncertainties about them, share them with a trusted and authentic friend. See how your friend reacts to your hopes and dreams. Be sure this person is reliable and will treat your hopes with the reverence and sincerity they deserve. A good friend can be very encouraging. The wrong kind of friend can pour doubt and discouragement on your hopes."

I was reluctant to break the spirit of the meeting by going for coffee and cookies, so I sat quietly on the chesterfield, thinking about and applying what the pastor had said. Kyle got up without saying a word and went to the coffee table. While he was gone, Jill came over and sat beside Karen and me. She was bubbling with excitement.

"I'm so excited," she said. "The pastor said to share your hopes with a trusted friend, and I thought immediately of you two. Allison, you helped me so much when I was discouraged and depressed. I want you to know that things have changed for me. I feel again that I want to devote my life to medical missionary work. This seems to be what God is calling me to, and I know I'd just love it and can think of nothing I'd rather devote my life to. I know it's a long way off yet, but I'm going to begin. I'm going to apply to enter medical school next fall. I want to get started to prepare myself. It seems that I now have a purpose and a reason for living. So," Jill said rather hesitantly, "what do you think? Do you think this is right for me?"

My heart went out to her. She seemed so sincere and happy, and her happiness affected me. I put my arm around her and said with enthusiasm, "Yes, Jill. I think this is just right for you. Go for it. Pursue it. You started out on this course once before and got sidetracked. Don't let anything or anyone sidetrack you again."

Even though Jill seemed to be speaking mainly to me, Karen nodded her head and agreed. "Yes, Jill, I think this is just right for you. There's a long road ahead, but I know you can do it and you'll persevere at it. And for you I can say, 'what better way to invest your life.'

We all became rather emotional at this point, but it was an emotion of happiness and joy at seeing someone pick up their life again and get going on a path that was right for them. I suddenly realized that I hadn't felt that happy in a long time ... if ever. I looked over at my best friend, Karen.

"What about you, Karen? Are your hopes and dreams still the same?"

"Yes," she said. "In fact, I feel they're being confirmed and that they're right for me." She looked at Jill. "I told Allison the other day that I don't have any great ambitions for a career, or a life of service in another country. I feel only a longing to be content and to make a happy and warm home for someone I love and to raise children. I feel as if God is saying that for me this will be a great value and great satisfaction. I also want to work with girls who have an unwanted pregnancy. Does it sound rather tame and lacking in ambition to you?"

Before Jill could answer I blurted out, "Of course not, Karen. We're all built and made for different things. Didn't the pastor say that the secret is to build your hopes in a way that fits your personality and your gifts? You'd be a wonderful person for this. You could have a long and fulfilling life, and be a blessing to those you love as well."

Jill nodded in support. "Absolutely, Karen! I've known you for a long time, and I know you would fit that dream beautifully."

I could see that Karen was touched by our responses. "Do you really think so? I sometimes wonder if I should be looking for something grander, or be striving to achieve something great with my life, but really that's not where by heart lies."

"Then follow your heart." I said with feeling. "But just continue to be my friend."

Karen suddenly reached out to me. "But what about you, Allison? What are your hopes and dreams? What do you want to do that you can pursue and follow with faith and trust?"

I'd been so absorbed in Jill and Karen's stories that I'd forgotten about my own dreams and hopes. "You know, Karen, this is all so new to me. I still don't know what to say in answer to your question. But I know there's something there. I'll keep on seeking and looking, but right now I don't know what it is. When I discover it, I'll tell you."

At this point Kyle returned with a tray-full of coffee and cookies. "Okay, you crowd, let's break this up and enjoy some coffee."

As I reached for the coffee I thought to myself that this had been one of the most significant evenings of my life. But its significance was only beginning. After some good conversation over coffee and cookies, the meeting began to break up and people began to leave. Karen and I rose to make our way to the car. As we said good night to Jill and Kyle, Kyle pulled me aside.

"Allison," he said, "why don't you come to church with us on Sunday morning. You can hear the pastor speak on this subject again, and then after church I'd like to invite you out for dinner."

I was very pleased with the invitation and readily agreed.

"It's a date then," said Kyle.

On the drive home I told Karen about Kyle's invitation.

"Kyle's a very nice person," she said. "Do you want this to develop?"

I was rather evasive in my answer. "I'm afraid because he doesn't know about my background. He has no idea of my previous life, and he doesn't know about the abortion. He seems to have been involved in Christian circles all his life and has been a good churchman. I don't know how he would react if I told him about my former life."

"There's only one way to find that out," replied Karen. "You'll have to tell him, and then we'll know how he reacts."

"If we go out for dinner after church, that'll give me a good opportunity to explain myself to him," I said.

It had been a full evening, and when I got home I wanted to go right to my bedroom to think about all that had happened, but my father was waiting for me and wanted to talk.

"How did the Bible study go tonight?" he asked.

"It was really very good," I responded, trying not to sound too enthusiastic.

He nodded his head in approval. "I want you to know that I've scheduled another luncheon meeting with the pastor and Jim Dexter. We'll be meeting next Tuesday again."

This greatly surprised me, and I waited for him to expand on what he said.

"I've given some things a great deal of thought since your mother died," he said. "All my life I've never given God or spiritual things much attention. They just didn't seem to be important to me. My mind has been focused on my career, making money, and providing for you and your mother. But since your mother died, I've had some questions. Where is she? Does she still exist? Is there life after death? Is she aware of us now, and is she watching what is happening to us? I have lots of questions, but I've pushed them to the back of my mind. There were so many other things to think about. But now I think it's time to face them and to ask them. Having met Jim and the pastor, I have confidence that they'll give me some honest and balanced answers."

"That sounds very good," I responded. This very neutral response was really an attempt to sound bland and rather none committal, but in fact it hid a rush of emotions that flooded me as I became aware of my father's sudden interest in spiritual things. "I hope you find answers to your questions; I think I'm beginning to find the answers to mine."

I didn't want the conversation to go beyond this point, so I protested that I was really very tired and needed to go to bed. I went up the stairs, closed the bedroom door, and realized that I had a great deal to think about—and pray about.

SECTION III
Love: The Lead Singer

CHAPTER TWELVE

THE CALL

Karen, Kyle, and I met again for lunch at the university cafeteria on Thursday. Since both Kyle and Karen seemed to be fairly well set about their dreams and hopes for the future, I felt a little out of things. I was still in a state of uncertainty and confusion. I knew that I wanted to do something meaningful with my life. I wanted to have strong hopes to pursue, but it wasn't clear what these hopes should be. My two friends, however, had some clear suggestions to make.

"Allison, I've not known you very long, but I've noticed this," Kyle said. "You have a strong intuitive understanding of other people. You're keenly aware when others have a problem, and you desire to immediately focus on their problem, understand it, and give them support and guidance. For example, I've known Jill in the Bible study group for a long time, but you seemed to form an immediate connection with her. She confided in you. She felt that you understood. She sensed you were listening to her and grasped just what she was going through. When you gave advice and guidance, she was confident that you knew what you were talking about. So I wondered, when it comes to your hopes and dreams if you should not think of some kind of counseling. I think you'd be very good at it."

"You know, I believe Kyle's right," said Karen. "Did you notice how Edgar gravitated to you at the meeting last Tuesday? He knew a lot of people in that group—people who knew him better than you. But it was you he seemed to focus on, and he came to you to talk."

"Yes," I replied, "but what I said to him was rather forceful, and I felt a little embarrassed after I'd said it."

"You said it because you had an understanding and insight into what his problem was," Kyle said. "You sensed the need behind his words and questions, and you had the courage to point it out to him in a gentle but clear way. Edgar needed to hear what you said, and I think he knew it."

Karen added, "Yes, I thought you were rather blunt with Edgar, but after you were finished I realized that was exactly what he needed to hear. You helped him in a way that no one else could. Besides, I know from my own experience that I can talk to you. You listen, you understand, and you seem to have insights that escape me. I think you have the heart and spirit to really reach out to hurting and confused people, understand them, and see solutions for them. I agree with Kyle. I think you should consider developing these gifts. You could help a lot of people.

As these friends of mine spoke, I felt a strange fire kindle in my heart. I yearned to do what they were saying I could do.

"Do you really think I could do that?" I asked, hoping for confirmation and support.

"Certainly," said Kyle.

"I think you have the natural heart and spirit for it," said Karen. "A lot of it comes naturally to you, but if you were to get some training and experience, you could become a very effective counsellor."

I was overcome by a strange feeling. It was as if a new vision was forming in my heart. *Was this for me? Was this the direction I was searching for?* I was being possessed with a new sense of excitement and recognition. My heart seemed to be saying *Yes! This is the direction for you. This is your hope. This is your vision.*

I was so overwhelmed by these new thoughts and emotions that I was speechless.

"I think you should pray about it and think about it," said Kyle.

"I will," I promised.

"And we'll pray for you, too," said Karen. "This may be the beginning of a whole new journey for you. You may have discovered your hopes and purpose. We'll certainly pray that God will make this clear to you."

"But where do I go from here?" I asked.

Kyle seemed to know what to say. "If this is the basic hope for your life, you have to accept it, entertain it, and commit yourself to it. Then you need to pass it on to the department of faith and start doing something about it. Look for opportunities to help and counsel people. That'll come naturally to you. And God knows there are innumerable people in the world with problems. So begin to look for opportunities. If no opportunities come your way, I'd question the authenticity of the gift. But if people come and share with you their deepest struggles and trust you with their most intimate feelings, and you're able to empathize with them and understand what they're going through and you give sound suggestions as to what they can do, then that's a good indication that other people recognize the gift in you. Once that happens and you've helped some people, you'll know from your own inner satisfaction that this area of service is right for you. It will give you fulfillment. You will sense happiness and peace in doing it."

"But I haven't had any training in this," I objected.

"Then, you may have to start thinking in terms of changing your university studies so that you get the training and knowledge that'll help you in this service. I know you're training for optometry, but if you become convinced that your hopes and dreams for service lie in another direction, then you may have to consider changing your study program. You have your hopes, now you need to have faith and begin to do the things that are necessary if your hopes are to be realized.

I thanked my friends for their help and guidance. I knew something significant had happened and the direction and meaning of my life had turned a meaningful corner. A new direction had opened up for me. The purpose and meaning of my life were beginning to reveal themselves to me.

We talked some more about the Bible study meetings and our hopes and faith for the future, but my mind and heart were racing in other directions, so I let Kyle and Karen do most of the talking. As we were leaving, Kyle reminded me of our date for the coming Sunday. We made arrangements to meet at the church and then go out for dinner after the service. I wondered if he would extend the invitation to include Karen, but he didn't. Apparently he wanted to go with me alone.

CHAPTER THIRTEEN

THE FOUR LOVES

I had mixed feelings about attending church on Sunday. I'd been to church before on a few occasions, but it had never been a significant part of my life. I realized it was one of those things that religious people did, but for me it seemed quite irrelevant to the substance and direction of my life up to that point.

Kyle met me at the church door and introduced me to a few people. Then he led me to a seat in the central section of the church sanctuary. The church was modestly designed with tasteful colours, decoration, and furniture. The wooden pews all faced the front towards a rather large platform. A central pulpit, seats for the choir, and an organ and piano at either side graced the platform.

The content of the service was new to me. I was unacquainted with most of the hymns we sang, but I did notice that the people sang them with great earnestness and enthusiasm. There was a contemporary flavour to the music, which pleased me. The service was conducted more informally than I'd experienced the few times I'd attended churches in the past. The relaxed nature of the service encouraged a friendly atmosphere of warmth and acceptance that I found quite comforting.

The central piece in the service was the message by the pastor. He continued his series of sermons on the dynamic trio of hope, faith, and love. That morning he spoke about love. I found what he said to be both interesting and enlightening. He presented the meaning of love in a different and refreshing way that certainly made it more understandable. He said that the meaning of the word love had become very broad in our culture, and we used it to mean almost anything that we thought was nice or likeable. We use the same word when we say "I love chocolate" as when we declare "I love my wife." It's the same word, but obviously with very different meanings. We could say "I love dogs" or "I love God." Again, it's the same word, but with vastly different concepts. The word love can describe just about anything we are fond of.

Clearly we need to have a much sharper understanding of what the Bible really means when it talks about love. I understood from what the pastor said that most of the early Bible manuscripts of the New Testament were written in Greek, and in the Greek language there are four words that are translated into English as *love*, but each word described a different type of love. Most of his sermon focused on describing these four different types of love. As I listened, I realized that a lot of my thoughts about love were sentimental, idealistic, and a little sloppy. God's love and the love described in the Bible were not at all what I imagined them to be. *There is so much I have to learn*, I thought. *There is so much I don't know.*

The pastor explained that the Greek word *eros* depicted a certain facet of love, namely the physical, sensual type of love. This is essentially a sexual attraction. Eros refers to the attraction of the sexes and the arousing of bodily desire and enjoyment in close physical contact. Often what is called love between the sexes is made up largely of eros love. Eros is the base for romantic love.

The second word for love is *philia*, which is the love that describes friendship. It may have no sexual connotation at all. There are people in the world with whom you have an affinity; they attract you, and you build a friendship with them. This type of love can extend to people of both sexes. It's the feeling that you can enjoyably associate with them because you have mutual interests and values. Philia is a sense of comradeship. This feeling of love can indeed become very strong and meaningful.

Storge is another word used in the Greek to describe love. This refers more to family love, such as the love of a father or mother for their children, the love of children for their parents, or the love of brothers and sisters. It's the natural affection for those who are our kin.

The word used most often in the New Testament for love is *agape*. This love rises above sexual attraction, mutual liking, or family affiliation. It's the kind of love God has towards us. It's the love of benevolence. When you love like this, you want to do good for others. You want to do what is best for them. Agape love says, "regardless of your attitude or actions towards me, I want good to come to you, so I'll work towards that end. This kind of love is more a function of the will than a natural feeling that arises in our hearts. We may not feel like doing the loving thing, but we do it anyway.

The love of benevolence can be extended to those outside the family circle or to people you may not naturally like. The pastor made a strong point that this love is extended to everyone. In fact, Jesus encourages us to even love our enemies. You may not be naturally attracted to your enemies, but in your heart you can still wish good for them and work for their benefit. With this type of love in your heart, you can do good to those who don't do good to you. You can bless those who curse you. You can look out for the good of others and work for their benefit, even though you will not get any benefit out of it yourself. This kind of love is unconditional. It does not say, "If you do good to me, I'll do good to you." It says, "Regardless of your attitudes or actions towards me, I'll have good will towards you and plan and act for your good."

The pastor emphasized that agape love is the kind of love God has towards us. When the Bible says that God is love, this is the kind of love it's talking about. When the Bible says God loved the world, it's referring to this kind of love. God loves us even in our sin and selfishness and disregard for Him. The Bible says that: *"God demonstrates his own love for us in this: While we were still sinners, Christ died for us."*[32] He reaches out to us and wishes the very best for us, even if we neglect Him and are indifferent towards Him. God's love is wonderful. He works for our good and seeks to accomplish our redemption and bring us back into fellowship with Him. The highest expression of this love towards us is through Jesus Christ. He seeks to win our hearts and allegiance through Jesus Christ. This is the love of God. This is a divine love. It doesn't come to us naturally. In fact, unless God gives it, we don't have it. The only way we can experience this genuine love is if God shares it with us. The Bible says this *"And hope does not disappoint us, because God has poured out his love into our hearts by the Holy Spirit, whom he has given us."*[33]

The pastor explained that the apostle Paul gave a great description of what this divine love is like when it gets hold of our hearts and our lives. He quoted from 1Corinthians chapter thirteen, which I'd heard before, even though my exposure to the Bible had been very limited.

---

32 Romans 5:8
33 Romans 5:5

Love is patient, love is kind. It does not envy, it does not boast, it is not proud. It is not rude, it is not self-seeking, it is not easily angered, it keeps no record of wrongs. Love does not delight in evil but rejoices with the truth. It always protects, always trusts, always hopes, always perseveres.[34]

The pastor concluded his remarks by saying, "When your heart is filled with this divine love, you'll notice that it has two sides. There is a cleansing side, because when this love rules in your life there is an absence of all unloving attitudes. Paul says it does not envy or boast, nor is it proud and rude. On the other hand, this love has a positive side. When it's in the heart, positive attitudes abound. It's patient and kind. This love is full of trust, hope, and perseverance. My hope and prayer for you all is that the love of God will reign in your hearts and lives."

This message from the pastor deeply impressed me. I knew that I'd had experiences of love in my life. I believed there were some people that I loved. I knew I'd experienced love from my parents. I was aware that there were things in the world that I liked and enjoyed, but the presence and quality of this divine love had been absent in my life. I knew there were people I resented. I especially resented the father of my aborted child. I was bitter at how easily he had refused any responsibility and left me to deal with the situation alone. I was still disappointed and rather angry with my old friends who deserted me so easily when I got in trouble. Even with my father I knew there was a residue of anger and resentment there for which I had no good reason. There were some people for whom I would find it very hard to work for their good; in fact, I would secretly enjoy seeing them knocked down a notch or two. I knew there were situations in which I wasn't patient, and there were people to whom I had not been kind. I knew that this quality of love didn't rule in my heart.

I left the church service understanding that this spiritual life was a dynamic, life changing affair, and not the casual attending of church once in a while. If I ever invited God into my life, then He would change things powerfully. He had a spiritual energy and power that would impact me and would make me a very different but better person. Did I want this change? Was I ready for this change?

The meal with Kyle was very pleasant. We seemed to enjoy one another's company. Conversation was free and smooth, and we communicated

---

34 1 Corinthians 13:4-7

with each other easily. I knew I had to let Kyle know that my past life had not been all sweetness and light. When the time came to do this, I actually found it was rather easy, as Kyle seemed to understand and sympathize. Once I got going with my story, I found that I was telling him much more than I had originally planned. I told him about the death of my mother and what a devastating blow that had been for me. I explained that I turned a lot of my resentment and anger about this towards my father. I knew it was unjust and that my father was doing his best, but I still felt alienated from him. I told Kyle about my wild years, when I lived for parties and fun, but below the surface I was really hurting and empty. He seemed to understand this.

Then I came to my pregnancy and abortion. I wondered how he would react to this and what kind of attitude he would have. Would this change his estimation of me? Would he reject me because of this? I told him everything. I explained about the emotional distress I went through at the loss of my baby. The loneliness. The guilt. The emptiness as my friends forsook me. I told him of my thoughts about suicide, but that I was a coward and didn't have the courage to go through with it. I explained how during this time of distress and loneliness Karen had gone out of her way to become my friend and had led me to the Bible study classes. I assured him that since attending the classes I was feeling challenged and excited about these new friends and the new way of life that was being revealed to me.

When I finished I was almost afraid to look at him. Would he disapprove of me? Would he be disillusioned that I was not the kind of person he thought I was? Could he associate freely with someone who had gone so far astray from the type of life that he espoused? How would he react? Would he want to start distancing himself from me? Would he be glad that he found this out early in our association, so that he could still withdraw with honour? I realized that Kyle's response to the unsavoury part of my life was very important to me.

I lifted my head and looked across the table at him. He was staring at me with deep concentration. He didn't respond at once but was silent for a while. I waited tensely for his answer. When I looked at his face, I could see that he was deeply moved, and that my story had affected him. But what I saw in his face was not rejection or judgment. Finally, he leaned across the table.

"Allison," he said quietly, "thank you for telling me all of that. I know it must have been difficult for you to tell your story. I can see the depth of hurt and distress you've come through, and I feel privileged that you felt free to share so much of yourself with me."

"I've never been able to share this with anyone else except Karen," I said. "You must think I'm a terrible person."

I watched as a smile began to form on Kyle's face. I'd never been so relieved to see someone smile instead of frown in my whole life. Hope began to come. Relief filled my heart. A burden seemed to begin to lift. *He's not going to reject me. He's not going to look for a graceful way out of this.*

With gentle earnestness he said, "Allison, what's really important is not what was in the past, but what's in the future. What really counts is not what you were, but what you're going to be. The wonderful thing about the love of God is that He's most willing to forgive the past and count it as forgotten. He can change our direction and get us moving in a new direction. It's as if He wipes the chalk board of our lives clean and eliminates all that was written there and gives us a fresh slate. We begin to write a new story as a new person, with new values and new commitments."

"Do you really think God will do that for me?" I asked.

"Yes!" Kyle exclaimed. "Jesus described it as being born again. He can change what we are in our hearts and we become like a new person. We're born again to start a new life as a new person. He's done that for me and I know He can do it for you."

As he spoke I realized how deeply I wanted this new life and to be a new person. I wanted to be forgiven for the past and to be given the strength and spirit to start out as a whole new person in a whole new life. I realized I wanted to put the old life behind me and reach out and grasp a new life.

"I want that, Kyle; pray for me that I may find this life soon."

By the time the meal was finished both of us felt that we had established a bond and had a better understanding of each other. On my way home I felt like my heart would burst with happiness. When last did I feel like this? Had I ever felt like this?

CHAPTER FOURTEEN

THE FELLOWSHIP

The day of the next Bible study came quickly. I found myself looking forward to the evening with keen anticipation. I felt I was coming to a crisis and would soon have to make some crucial decisions about God and my spiritual life. A whole new world was opening up to me. This included my spiritual search for a relationship with God, my consideration of a whole new direction for my career, and my relationship with Kyle. I was beginning to understand there were truths and dynamics in living for God that I hadn't realized were there. Part of me was anxious to reach out and grasp this new life, while another part of me was afraid and hesitated to leave what was familiar in order to venture into this new experience. I had gone along this path far enough to know that soon I would have to make a decision. Was I going to follow God and live for Him? Was I going to embrace the realities of the spiritual life, or was I going to reject these beckoning values and return to what I had always relied upon to fill my life with meaning?

I listened carefully to the pastor as he began the study. He had a little smile on his face and a twinkle in his eye as he began. "I think most of you were at church on Sunday morning, so I don't need to go into the meaning of love and the four loves that are part of the Greek language." With a broader smile he continued. "And I know you were all listening intently and can remember everything that I said." We all knowingly smiled back at him and nodded our heads. "When I speak of love in the Christian life, I'm talking about agape love, divine love, the type of love that God has. It's the love of benevolence and good will and can operate in our hearts, even towards people we don't necessarily like. We seek for the good and for the benefit of others, even those who seem to be trying to harm us or cause us pain." Again, we all agreed with this review of his Sunday morning sermon. We understood the type of love he was talking about.

"Keeping that in mind, I want to talk about this kind of love tonight … how it operates in our hearts and the difference it makes in our attitudes and way of living. First, however, I want to remind you that this love is part of a dynamic trio. We're talking about the cooperative functions of hope, faith, and love. These three qualities work together. They support and encourage one another. They don't do well on their own. They harmonize well with each other, but are poor performers as soloists." Again, we all agreed with this reminder.

"When we think of hope, faith, and love as a dynamic trio, we need to understand that love emerges as the lead singer. The other two are in a supportive role, but the real melody is carried by love. In the heart of the Christian person, love is predominant, just as it is in the heart of God. It's vital to understand that the dominant quality operating in the character and being of God is the spirit of holy love, and this holy love is reflected in the life and character of all who are in true fellowship with God. I'd like to quote a number of verses from the Bible that emphasize the essential nature of love in the life of a Christian."

The pastor took up his Bible and continued. "The Apostle Paul makes an important statement in his first letter to the Corinthians when he says: '*And now these three remain: faith, hope and love. But the greatest of these is love.*'[35]

"All three of these qualities are essential for a rich and victorious Christian life, but the most important is the spirit of agape love."

Referring to his Bible again, the pastor continued. "Jesus also emphasized the predominance of love when someone asked him what the most important commandment was. His answer was immediate:

"The most important one," answered Jesus, "is this: 'Hear, O Israel, the Lord our God, the Lord is one. Love the Lord your God with all your heart and with all your soul and with all your mind and with all your strength.' The second is this: 'love your neighbor as yourself.' There is no commandment greater than these."[36]

---

35 1 Corinthians 13:13
36 Mark 12:29–31

"Jesus made it clear how essential love was for those who are His followers when He said to the disciples just before his crucifixion:

A new command I give you: Love one another. As I have loved you, so you must love one another. By this everyone will know that you are my disciples, if you love one another.[37]

"The Apostle Peter joins the chorus about love when he instructs the early Christians: *"Now that you have purified yourselves by obeying the truth so that you have sincere love for each other, love one another deeply, from the heart."*[38]

"The Apostle John is rather blunt and forceful about the subject. He leaves us in no doubt when he says:

Dear friends, let us love one another, for love comes from God. Everyone who loves has been born of God and knows God. Whoever does not love does not know God, because God is love.[39]

"I think you can see from these verses," said the pastor, "that love for God and love for others is the natural outcome of any meaningful fellowship and interaction with God. If His spirit is in our hearts, we will love from our hearts, for God is love. Love is the essence, the hallmark, of being close to God. Love is the lead singer in this dynamic trio.

"Since we're quoting from the Bible, let me add to this by pointing out that true agape love for God and others is linked in the Bible with obedience to God. This is important, because it shows the nature of this love. Agape is more than nice feelings about God and others. It goes beyond our sentimentalities and emotions; this love reaches into the operating centre of our being and deeply affects our will, intentions, and purposes. If we truly love God, we will obey Him. Jesus said it plainly, *'If you love me, you will obey what I command.'*[40]

"He also said:

---

37 John 13:34–35
38 1 Peter 1:22
39 1 John 4:7–8
40 John 14:15

On that day you will realize that I am in my Father, and you are in me, and I am in you. Whoever has my commands and obeys them, he is the one who loves me. He who loves me will be loved by my Father, and I too will love him and show myself to him.[41]

"The apostle John repeats the same sentiment, indicating that love is more than emotion. It expresses itself in willing obedience to God.

This is how we know that we love the children of God: by loving God and carrying out his commands. In fact, this is love for God: to keep his commands. And his commands are not burdensome.[42]

As I listened to this, I wasn't comfortable. My conscience was pricking me. I had not loved God. In fact, I had badly neglected Him. He may have loved me, but I'd exhibited little or no interest in Him. I couldn't say in any real way up to this point in my life that I'd loved God, and I certainly hadn't obeyed His commandments, nor had I even felt any interest in obeying Him. It was also true that my love for other people was rather spotty. I liked and enjoyed some people, but not all. My love for others seemed to be determined by whether or not I liked them. Although I didn't want to admit it, there were some people that I just couldn't stand, and some I even harboured bitterness and resentfulness against. If what the pastor was saying was true, then I was not in touch with God. His Spirit was not in me. This realization deeply distressed me. I felt that I really did want God in my life. I wanted to love Him and know Him, but where did this love come from, and how could I get it? The next point in the pastor's talk made me even more uncomfortable.

"The next thing I want to emphasize about this love is that it's the love of God. It's supernatural love. Humans can't produce or develop it on their own without God. This is a love that only God can give. To put it bluntly, if God doesn't give it, then you don't have it. You cannot work hard to get it into your heart. You cannot by your earnestness or efforts produce it. The human heart does not have the ability to start to love like this. This love exists beyond the strength of human effort. I say it again ... if God doesn't give it, you don't have it. If you have it, it's because you've

41 John 14:20–21
42 1 John 5:2–3

been in contact with God, and His spirit has infused your spirit with His love. If Jesus is in your heart, this love will be there. If He's not in your heart, this love is not in there. This love flows from God to us, but for us to receive it, there must be contact and fellowship with God. John tells us:

Dear friends, since God so loved us, we also ought to love one another. No one has ever seen God; but if we love one another, God lives in us and his love is made complete in us.[43]

"This is God's love. If God is in us, we will love like this. On our own we cannot manufacture love like this."

Jim Dexter spoke up at this point. "Isn't this relationship what Jesus was illustrating when He used the example of a vine and its branches? He said that the branch must stay connected to the stem of the vine or it will wither and die. The branch by itself has no power or ability to produce fruit. It must stay in close contact with the vine. When that contact is there, the nourishment and life of the vine flow into the branch and produce fruitfulness. When that connection is severed, the branch will die. The branch doesn't produce fruit on its own without the vine."

"Well said," responded the pastor. "In fact, the relationship between the branches and the vine is so intimate that Jesus carries the illustration a step farther. It's like living in each other. He lives in us; we live in Him, just like branches and vines are entwined together:

I am the vine, you are the branches. If you remain in me and I in you, you will bear much fruit; apart from me you can do nothing. If you do not remain in me, you are like a branch that is thrown away and withers; such branches are picked up, thrown into the fire and burned.[44]

"Jesus goes on to say:

As the Father has loved me, so have I loved you. Now remain in my love. If you keep my commands, you will remain in my love, just as I have kept my Father's commands and remain in his love.[45]

---

43 1 John 4:11–12
44 John 15:5–6
45 John 15:9–10

"You can see the picture Jesus is painting here. We receive the spirit of love flowing into us from Him. If we don't receive this from Him, we don't have the ability to produce it on our own. We receive it by living in Him, and Him living in us. This close fellowship and absorbing of God's Spirit brings His love into our lives.

"The apostle Paul states it quite clearly when he says: '*And hope does not put us to shame, because God has poured out his love into our hearts by the Holy Spirit, who has been given to us.*'[46]

"This is God's love. It's a supernatural love. God wants to share it with us, but this happens only when we are in close fellowship with Him. We absorb it from Him. It flows into us from Him. Without this inner fellowship and connection, the stream of His love doesn't flow. Love is a part of the dynamic trio, and it's the lead voice. Love is the predominant Christian virtue. Divine love is supernatural; we cannot produce it on our own. We receive it from God."

A strange and awesome spirit seemed to pervade the whole group. No one spoke; in fact, no one even moved. Everyone seemed to be caught up in intense concentration. We were standing face to face with an awesome truth that stunned and overwhelmed us. The pastor, sensing the spirit of the moment, said, "I'd like us right now to spend time in quiet, personal prayer and meditation. Try to sense God's presence. Let His Spirit come to you. Let His love flow into you. If you have any unloving attitude towards anyone, let the love of God melt that hardness and warm that coldness into accepting love. Reach out now in your heart and sense God's nearness and presence in your life, and let His love and life flow freely into your heart and soul."

The atmosphere in the group was profound. I tried to do what the pastor said, but I was quite inexperienced at this kind of inner awareness. I wanted God's presence in my heart, but lacked the spiritual sensitivity to know whether it was there or not. I longed for close fellowship with Him, and I certainly needed His love to flow into me, but I was powerless to make this happen, in spite of all of my earnestness and desires. The silence in the group continued. I was aware that although there was no sound, intense communication was taking place. *How could silence be so profound?* I thought.

---

46 Romans 5:5

The quietness was so rich, I was a little disappointed when the pastor called for our attention again and began to speak.

"Love does much more for us, but I think it would be good to have a break now before we consider some of the other things that the quality of love does in our hearts and lives. Let's have some coffee and cookies."

As soon as the break was announced, and even before we had a chance to get some coffee, Edgar came over again to speak to us. He sat down, looked at me, and without any preamble said, "I want you to know, Allison, that I thought you were a little hard on me at the last meeting. What you said was rather pointed and difficult for me to accept. But I've thought about it, and I realized that what you were saying was the truth. Over the past few days as I considered your comments, it began to dawn on me that I was spiritually lazy. I want to experience all of the blessings and benefits, but I don't want to go to great efforts, or make significant sacrifices, to see them happen. I want it to come easily and without discomfort or sacrifice on my part. The idea I had of faith was that if I just asked in faith, God would do all kinds of nice things for me. I now realize that my unwillingness to go to any great bother or inconvenience is spiritual laziness. What you said pierced my conscience, and I realized that I was in error. I want to thank you for understanding me and for saying what needed to be said. It must have been difficult for you, but you had the courage to say it, and I thank you for it."

I thanked Edgar for his honesty, and as he left to go to the refreshment table, I sat back a little stunned. Kyle was not stunned.

"See," he said, "there's someone else you've helped. You helped Jill, and you helped Edgar. You're only new to the group, they hardly know you, and yet already they sense that they can come to you and be understood and accepted. I think you have a gift that you should develop."

"I agree," said Karen. "You've not only helped them, but you've helped me as well. I think that God could use you to understand and counsel other people who have deep needs. You sometimes see in us what we don't see in ourselves, and you're able to define it and articulate it for us. Perhaps this is the direction in life God wants you to go."

All of this pleased and excited me. I'd been thinking about what Karen and Kyle had said to me during the past Thursday's lunch. In fact, I'd even prayed about it in my own way. There was no doubt that this concept of helping others in their personal lives was something that excited me. I didn't know whether I had a gift for it or not, but I did know that when I thought about it, my heart leaped and my spirit was stirred. Could I do this effectively? I was becoming aware that there had never been anything else that had given me the sense of purpose, calling, and satisfaction as this did. Could I hope for this? Could I believe that here was where my purpose and calling lay? Was I willing to change my course in life and begin to train for this sort of work and ministry? Was this where my hope and faith were supposed to be applied? I knew in my heart that I could very happily commit myself to this sort of work. And what about divine love? I could certainly see how true divine love and caring could operate effectively in this way.

We went to get coffee and had some pleasant conversation with other members of the group that I hadn't had opportunity to talk with before. I was feeling increasingly comfortable with these people. I seemed to be fitting in more and more, and their openness and sincerity appealed to me. But I did wonder how they would react if they knew the kind of life I'd been living. Would they all be as kind and understanding as Kyle?

I knew that my father had met with the pastor and Jim Dexter for lunch again that day. He was working late, so I hadn't been able to find out from him how the lunch went. Jim came to me, however, and casually said that he'd enjoyed the lunch with my father.

"He's a very thoughtful man," said Jim. "I really enjoyed his company."

That was all, but I had the feeling there was much more he could have said, but didn't. I made note that I would have to take time when I got home to talk to my father about the lunch.

CHAPTER FIFTEEN

THE CLEANSING

The pastor called us back together for the next part of his presentation.

"We're talking about hope, faith, and love as a dynamic trio. Love is the dominant member of the trio, but we ourselves cannot produce this kind of divine love no matter how earnestly we try. It's a supernatural love and flows into us from God in response to our faith and obedience to Him.

"This love is a powerful thing, and its presence in our hearts influences all other parts of our living. Let's look at some of the other benefits this love brings into our hearts. First, this divine love helps purify our hopes and our faith. When you stop to think about it, it would be very easy for us to establish selfish hopes and have dreams that would feed our pride. We could be very worldly and fleshly in the things we hope for. Given the sinful propensity of the human heart, it would be natural for us to manufacture hopes and dreams that are far outside of the will of God. We could be hoping for our own glory and dreaming for our own benefit. We could certainly believe in these selfish dreams and work hard to fulfill them. We could try to use the principles of hope and faith for our own selfish ends. This is a corruption of hope and faith and is not worthy of them, but it does happen."

One of the men interrupted. "I've been wondering about this as I listened to your teaching on hope and faith. I wondered what's to stop us being selfish and greedy, or worldly in our hopes and dreams and then working hard to see them fulfilled, even though they are unworthy of God and not in His will."

"Right," someone else said. "I've been wondering the same thing. I'm sure Adolph Hitler had great hopes and dreams about what he wanted to accomplish, and he worked hard to achieve them. But in the absence of love, these dreams caused untold suffering, damage, and death."

The pastor nodded. "These are good thoughts, and you can see why one of the important functions of love is that it purifies our motives and cleanses our purposes so that our hopes and dreams are clean and pure and motivated out of a heart of love for God and others. Divine love directs our hopes and faith in the direction of God's will and purposes. Hopes and dreams coming out of a selfish heart can be very different to the hopes and dreams that come out of a pure and loving heart. Even if the hopes we have are good, they can lose their power when our own selfishness and desire for prominence, wealth, or fame motivate them. Hope and faith can very quickly lose their way and move us in the wrong direction without the guiding and motivating hand of love. That is why the apostle Peter said:

> ...that your faith and hope might be in God. Seeing ye have purified your souls in obeying the truth through the Spirit unto unfeigned love of the brethren, see that you love one another with a pure heart fervently.[47]

"To keep this thing on track and not be side tracked by selfish motivations, we need to keep our faith and hope in God and be motivated by a pure heart of deep love."

"It's like a garden in which you plant seeds," one of the ladies added. "Hope and faith are like the soil in which they're planted. If the soil is good, then the seeds grow to strong maturity, but the kind of seed you plant determines what kind of plant is going to grow. The plants that grow from loving seeds will be fruitful and rich, but the plants that grow from selfish seeds can become harmful weeds."

"Yes," said someone else, "and since we're all going to love something, something is going to grow. The type of love you plant germinates into the kind of plant that will grow. If you love bad things, bad plants will grow. If you love good things, good plants will grow."

"Does that mean," someone interjected, "that you can hope for something good, but if you do it from the wrong motivation, then the value of it as a spiritual principle is lost?"

"Exactly," said the pastor. "That's what Paul was talking about in the great chapter on love when he said:

If I speak in the tongues of men or of angels, but do not have love, I am only a resounding gong or a clanging symbol. If I have the gift of prophecy and can fathom all mysteries and all knowledge, and if I have a faith that can move mountains, but do not have love, I am nothing. If I give all I possess to the poor and give over my body to hardship that I may boast, but do not have love, I gain nothing.[48]

"You can see that all of the things Paul is speaking about here are good. It's good to speak in tongues and to have faith that will move mountains. It's certainly good to give all your goods to feed the poor and be prepared to die for your faith. All of these things are good and to be applauded. But if these good things are done for selfish glory and false motivations and without love, then they're empty like a resounding gong or a clanging symbol. When they're not motivated by love, they lose their value in the Kingdom of God."

Someone with a frown on his face asked the next question. "But is this possible? Is it possible for us to act entirely out of love, without any element of selfishness or self interest there?"

"When Jesus told us to love God with all of our heart, all of our mind, all of our soul and all of our strength, He seemed to be encompassing our whole being. All means every part. Filled means there is no room for anything else. The fact that we love with all of our heart, and not just some of it, or part of it, implies the absence of any spirit that is contrary to love."

"But what if your motives are mixed?" the same person insisted. "You do love, and you want to help, but in helping there are also benefits that come to you. You act out of love, but also because there's personal benefit that comes to you. There's an element of self-interest."

"What is the predominant motivation?" asked the pastor. "To do it may well benefit you, but if you would do it anyway, out of love whether it benefits your or not, then the dominant motivation is love. If you see no benefit in it for yourself and decide not to do it, even if it helps the other person, then there is an absence of love."

---

48 1 Corinthians 13:1–3

Jim Dexter spoke up. "I think, pastor, that there's also a distinction to be made between self-interest and selfishness. When Jesus told us to love our neighbor as ourselves, He gave us room for proper self-interest. We should look after ourselves. Selfishness, on the other hand, means that our self-interest has become so dominant that it becomes the primary motive we follow, even if we hurt or neglect others."

As I listened to Jim I thought, *Here is a very wise and thoughtful man.*

"It seems to me," Jim continued, "that in nearly all of the decisions we make there are usually two or three different motivations. For example, I might decide to give a large sum of money to the church. That's a very generous act, but there could be a number of different motivations behind my generous act. The church may need the money, and I give because I love the church and want to help. It could be an act of love and obedience to God because I want to honour Him. I'm motivated out of a spirit of love. It's also possible that I realize when I give the money people will say 'look how generous Jim is. Isn't he a wonderful person?' I didn't give the money so that people would say that, but I'm pleased to know that people think well of me. Even more ungracious, it could be that I want to sit on the church board, and I give all that money to help me get elected, since everyone will think I have the interests of the church at heart. It seems to me that in every decision there could be a number of motivating factors. But if the predominant reason is love, I'll give the money even if no one knows I'm doing it. If I give it anonymously so it won't help to get me elected to the board, then the predominant motivation is love, not self-interest. In every decision there are always two or three factors, and the question is 'what is the primary one?'"

"That's right," said the pastor. "That's why Jesus said to seek first his kingdom and his righteousness, and all these things will be given to you as well.[49] The primary message is to put the values of His Kingdom first, and then the other things will be added to us. It's not that the other things have absolutely no value, or that we don't take them into consideration when we make decisions, but we put the first things first. Jim's right. In almost every decision we take a number of factors into consideration, but the predominant and deciding factor is love. Even though we realize there are costs and self-denials involved, we aren't deterred from doing what we're supposed to do."

---

49 Matthew 6:33

This was getting a bit beyond me. I felt confident enough, however, to insert my thoughts into the discussion at this point. "But who can be that good? Who can be that unselfish? I'd like to, but I can't."

"Nobody in their own strength can live like that, Allison," the pastor replied. "Nobody can love like this. Nobody, without the help of God, can let the agape love become so strong in his or her character that it conquers all other affections. That's why I said it's a supernatural love. God gives it. God's Spirit comes into our hearts and into our lives and spreads that love abroad. God fills us with His love and His grace. By ourselves we can't get rid of the selfish motives, but with God in our hearts and His love flowing in us, we can act out of loving and good motivations. Without God, we cannot do it.

"The Apostle John underlined the concept that this love comes to us from God, and if He's not in our lives and in our hearts, then this love does not operate in us. He said:

Dear friends, let us love one another, for love comes from God. Everyone who loves has been born of God and knows God. Whoever does not love does not know God, because God is love.[50]

"It's the presence of the Spirit of God in our lives that generates this kind of love. Without God's presence, we can't experience this type of love."

It must be wonderful to have the presence of God so real in your life that this love dominates the motives of our heart, I thought.

At this point, Jim Dexter, who seemed to be deeply involved in the subject, introduced a thought. "What you're saying about the love of God is certainly true when it comes to divine love. But the basic principles of hope, faith, and love, still apply when we're talking at the level of basic, human fleshly love—even sinful and carnal love. The human heart, whether it's pure or corrupt, is going to love something. If it's corrupt, it will love the wrong things, but it's going to love something. You could love money. You could love power. You could love pleasure. You could love pride and position. When you love the wrong things, you'll still pursue them, but they'll set your heart on the wrong track. They make you hope and wish for the wrong things. Some people fiercely love the wrong things and therefore develop wrong hopes. They then work hard to achieve these wrong

---

50 1 John 4:7–8

goals. The principles of faith and hope can still apply, even when the love is coming from a selfish and greedy or sinful heart. It seems to me the world is full of people who passionately love the wrong things, and from this wrong love they've developed false hopes. With great energy they work hard to achieve them, even if they're selfish, greedy, and worldly."

The pastor thought carefully about what Jim had said. "Yes, I think you're right. There are people who are passionately driven to seek selfish and greedy ends. They work hard at it. They become self-absorbed in it. They give a lot of time and energy to it. They'll even harm others in order to get what they want. Selfish, fleshly love is what many people live by."

"But isn't this what distinguishes Christians from everyone else?" someone asked.

"Yes, exactly," the pastor agreed. "What's different about Christians is that they sincerely love things that nobody else loves, and they have little affection for the things that seem so important to everybody else. That is why the Bible encourages us this way:

Do not love the world or anything in the world. If anyone loves the world, love for the Father is not in them. For everything in the world—the lust of the flesh, the lust of his eyes, and the pride of life—comes not from the Father but from the world. The world and its desires pass away, but whoever does the will of God lives forever.[51]

Jim Dexter persisted. "Yes, I can see that. The issue is not whether you're going to love or not. Everybody is going to love something. The issue is what are you going to love. Love of money, love of power, love of position, love of possessions, and love of self, are still loves, and many people love these things deeply. What makes the Christians so different is that what they love is very different. They love God supremely; they love others; they love God's will and God's glory. They love the needs of their soul above the needs of the body. They love first the Kingdom of God. This love grows and flowers into a whole different lifestyle. What we as Christians prize and value is entirely different. We put the Kingdom of God first. We seek and long for holiness of heart and purity of mind. We devote ourselves to different causes, and we prize what is true and genuine. This is what makes the Christian different."

---

51 1 John 2:15–17

"That's why people may think we Christians are a little strange," suggested one lady. "We fervently love things that others value very little, and we place little value on things that others love fervently. It all comes down to what you love, which is why Jesus keeps telling us to love God first and supremely and love our neighbour as ourselves. What really counts is what you love the most."

The pastor was quiet for a few moments. "I'm excited to see that you're grasping the basic principle that what counts the most is what you love. You can see why love is so important. It purifies what we hope for."

He paused again to give anyone else a chance to speak if they wished. When no one spoke he continued. "The next important thing that divine love brings into our lives is energy. I'm sure you've all experienced the power of love in your life. When you're in love, you experience a powerful energy. You feel alive. You feel you want to do something. It brings enthusiasm and meaning and intensity to living."

At this point one of the young men added some thoughts to the discussion. "I can testify to the truth of that." He turned and looked at his wife who was sitting beside him. "When I fell in love with Jenny, she happened to live a few miles away from me. I didn't have a car, so if I wanted to see her, I had to either cycle or walk. It was amazing to me how short and easy those miles were. I never felt they were too long or too tiresome. I had energy and enthusiasm, and I covered those miles gladly. But I noted that some of the other miles that I had to travel for other purposes were much longer and much more tiresome. Love motivates and gives strength and energy."

We all laughed at this, but we also agreed with him. Love seems to fill us with energy. Love helps us do things, achieve things, attempt things, and undertake things with a will and enthusiasm we wouldn't normally have the stamina or strength to undertake. Love brings strength and life to us.

The pastor also agreed. "Yes, when love fills the heart the world seems to come alive. We're filled with the enjoyment of living. There's purpose, joy, and enthusiasm. People who love God and love others have shown remarkable stamina in pursuing their objectives. They work harder, live more enthusiastically, appreciate the beauty of the world, and enjoy the thrills of living. They're alive and bright and filled with stamina and strength. Love indeed gives to us strength and energy. It propels us to an awareness of life that we never had before. I think the hymn-writer said it well when he wrote:

Heav'n above is softer blue;
Earth around is sweeter green;
Something lives in ev'ry hue
Christless eyes have never seen.
Birds with gladder songs o'er-flow;
Flow'rs with deeper beauties shine
Since I know, as now I know,
I am His, and He is mine.[52]

"In the same way," continued the pastor, "You can see that the energy and power of love is essential for the health of our hope and faith. Love intensifies our hopes, and that energizes our faith."

"Does that mean," one lady asked, "that if you love little, you'll want little, so you'll hope and attempt little? If you love intensely, will you want intensely, hope intensely, and try intensely? When a mother loves her child intensely, then she cares intensely. No effort is too great. No sacrifice is too much to help that child to a meaningful and fruitful life. The depth of your love determines the brightness of your hopes and the commitment of your faith to work for the realization of your hopes."

"Yes," someone else added, "I can see that. Love brings the strength and energy you'll need to keep working with faith for the realization of your hopes. When the way seems hard and discouraging, when the sacrifices seem too great and your strength seems to be failing, it's the power and energy of love that gives your faith the strength to carry on. If your love is weak, your hope and faith are weak. When difficulties, trials, and discouragements come, your faith will give up."

"Good!" said the pastor. "You're getting the idea. No wonder the Bible is constantly urging Christian to a deep, intense, full love for God and for others. Love is the power source from the Holy Spirit that keeps hope and faith functioning at top efficiency."

The pastor rested, took a breath and then continued quietly but earnestly. "But I'll tell you this—if the love of God is flowing in your lives, and you're bright with the hopes that His purpose has placed in your hearts, and if you're pursuing those hopes with faith and trust, then you are indeed living life and living it to the full. You're experiencing values

---

52 *I am His, and He is Mine*, George W. Robinson (1876)

and riches that can never be experienced by the selfish and greedy way of the world. This is life lived to the full. It's satisfying, joyful, and fulfilling."

The pastor closed his Bible. "I think that's enough for tonight. We can conclude this series on hope, faith, and love next week. If any of you have any comments to make or questions to ask you should bring them with you next week and we'll discuss them."

Looking at his watch, the pastor said, "We still have some time, so let's spend it in prayer. I think we have a lot to pray about."

I certainly felt that I had heard more than I could absorb in one night and appreciated the opportunity to think and pray over what I'd heard. I didn't participate in any of the open spoken prayers from the group, but I did pray earnestly in my heart, which seemed so empty of the type of love the pastor had been talking about.

Karen and I were in no hurry to go home after the meeting, so we joined the others for coffee and conversation. Kyle seemed relaxed and stayed with us. One lady in particular seemed anxious to strike up a conversation. Her name was Margaret. We hadn't talked long before she opened up and confided in us. She was having a problem at home. She was married with two small children, and was struggling with the discipline of her children, who were five and three. Her husband was deeply involved in his career and his work, so wasn't present with her that night. The two of them had different views about how to discipline the children. While Margaret wanted to discipline the children and give them rules to follow, her husband was much more unstructured and tended to give the children whatever they wanted. The children soon learned that if they wanted something, it was easier to get Father's permission, so they'd go to him. She disagreed with many of his decisions regarding the children. Since she was the homemaker and mother, she felt that her opinions should hold more weight than his did. It was causing problems not only with the children, but also between the husband and her.

I wondered why she was telling us this problem, since none of us were married or were looking after children. As she spoke, however, she seemed to increasingly unburden her concerns on me. I listened, and felt I understood what she was dealing with. I asked some questions about the children and her husband, which she readily answered. I could sense that she cared deeply about creating a good atmosphere in her home and was distressed at the tension. I sensed that what was really troubling her was the conflict building between her and her husband, so I gently spoke to this issue and focused our attention on that. She seemed relieved that she was able to speak about it, and we spent quite a long time talking together. At the end of the conversation she thanked me and said that it had helped her just to talk to someone about what was on her mind.

As Margaret left, Kyle said to me quietly, "There you go again. People can confide in you. She almost forgot that Karen and I were here."

"You seem to have a real gift here," Karen added. "People sense intuitively that you understand, that you'll not judge or condemn but will give them good direction. You're a natural counsellor."

I appreciated what they were saying and thanked them for their encouragement. I did, however, have some conflicting thoughts about the matter. I realized that I was excited and fulfilled in doing this, and it did seem to come quite naturally, but I also realized that if I pursued it, it would mean a whole new direction for me with different studies at the university. I wasn't too sure I was ready for such a dramatic change in the direction of my life, but I had to confess that this seemed to be where my heart lay. Was this where hope and faith and love were leading me? *Could I be satisfied to do this as an informed and casual hobby, or should I develop it as a profession?* I wondered.

When I got home, I knew that the evening was not yet finished. My father was there and clearly wanted to talk. Sensing this, I sat down with him and opened the conversation by asking about his lunch with Jim and the pastor.

He seemed to hesitate a little as if uncertain just how to proceed. He eventually said, "It went very well. I was very impressed with what they had to say. In fact," he said with even more hesitancy, "I'd like to go to church with you next Sunday."

This statement greatly surprised me and I was not at all certain how I should respond. My father had shown no interest in church or spiritual things, and I couldn't understand why he was showing this sudden interest. In fact, I felt suspicious. My suspicions made me wonder if his new-found interest was a genuine, personal spiritual hunger, or more of a curiosity about the group with which I was associating myself with. I wasn't sure if I wanted my father getting involved with my new friends.

The church and Bible study group were both so new to me. I was enjoying them, but I still had many questions and I wasn't sure yet how committed I wanted to be to them. At this point in my association, I didn't want my father expressing opinions on them, or passing judgments, especially when my own mind was still so fluid. I could, however, hardly reject the idea of him coming to church. In fact, I thought it might be a good way to introduce him to Kyle. He already knew Karen, so I responded in a way that I hoped would cover up my uncertainty.

"That would be good. In fact, there's a young man who goes to church that I want you to meet."

Father seemed relieved. "Good. Then why don't I invite Karen, your young gentleman friend, and you out for lunch next Sunday after church?"

"That would be great," I said.

It would be a good way for my father to get to know Kyle.

As I went to bed that night my thoughts were racing. Things are really changing. My life is opening up in a whole new direction. I feel a little frightened about these changes, but also a little excited and challenged. I prayed before going to bed and told God as best I could what was on my mind: *God, you're You're filling my heart with new hopes that are different from anything I've ever thought of before. If this is You talking to me, I'm excited and thrilled about these new directions. I'm also a little afraid that it could all be a delusion and I'll end up badly disappointed. I'm trying to believe in the hopes that You seem to be putting into my mind. If they aren't authentic, or if they're not for me, please let me know this in some way. If they are for me and they genuinely reflect what You want in my life, then help me to believe in them and do whatever I can to see them fulfilled. Please. I need your help.*

So I slept ... excited but peaceful.

Chapter Sixteen

The Message

I knew my life was changing. I could see many new doors opening up for me. I was anxious to take advantage of these new possibilities and follow where they may lead, but I didn't anticipate the life-changing experience that was to happen to me in the next day or two. It really started when I met with Kyle and Karen for our Thursday lunch.

After exchanging a few pleasantries, Kyle seemed determined to take charge of the conversation, and he was speaking to me.

"Allison," he said with purpose, "I think you have some very important decisions to make."

I was a little surprised at the strength of the statement and the abrupt change in the direction of the conversation, but I had to agree with him. I was being confronted with a whole new set of values and directions.

Kyle continued. "I think that it's God who's suggesting these changes. I think God wants to come into your life."

I protested a little bit to this forthright approach. "But I've not lived a good life. I've not bothered about God. How could He be interested in me?"

"You've heard the pastor speak about love and especially God's love. God loves you, Allison. He grieves over the life you've lived, but He's willing to forgive and change you. He wants to get you started on a new pathway in life."

"I'm beginning to realize that I need to take a different path in life, but would God really do that for me, even though I've been so indifferent to Him and done so much that I know He wouldn't approve of?"

"The reason I'm being so up front with you, Allison, is because I believe God is reaching out to you right now, and is willing to forgive all of the past and change you and change your life so that you can live for Him.

That's the wonderful story of the gospel, that God will redeem us through Jesus Christ— and that includes you. The Bible says, *"But God demonstrates his own love for us in this: While we were still sinners, Christ died for us."*[53]

"You mean that if I ask Him, God will forgive me for the past and will help me start a new life?"

"Yes. God can do that and has demonstrated His readiness to change us through the death and resurrection of Jesus Christ."

I knew that Kyle was deliberately steering me into territory that I was unfamiliar with, so I was still hesitant.

"It's true that I want a change in my life," I said. "I want to leave the old life. It's left me so empty and confused, and I don't want to go back and live as I've been living. Are you saying to me that God wants me to have a new life and He can help me find it, and this new life with Him will bring more meaning, purpose, and satisfaction to me?"

"Right," said Kyle.

"But I don't know how to do that, and I don't think I have the will-power to leave my old life and live for Him the way I should."

"Allison, you're correct; you don't have the will power. Nobody does. If we're going to live for Him, we have to trust Him to change us and give us the power and strength to live for Him so that we can embrace and enjoy the new life with Him. He gives it; we don't have it, nor can we achieve it on our own."

"Could this happen to me?"

"Yes, certainly it can. You know how many Christian denominations talk about baptism. Baptism is an outward, physical act that reflects the spiritual reality that takes place in our hearts when God redeems us."

Kyle took out a small New Testament from his pocket. "Let me read some verses to you." He turned the pages of his Bible until he came to the part that he wanted and read:

Or don't you know that all of us who were baptized into Christ Jesus were baptized into his death? We were therefore buried with him through baptism into death in order that, just as Christ was raised from the dead through the glory of the Father, we too may live a new life. For if we have been united with him like this in his death, we will certainly also be united with him in a resurrection like his. For we know that our old self was crucified with him so that the body ruled by sin might be done away with, that we should no longer be slaves to sin—because anyone who has died has been set free from sin. Now if we died with Christ, we believe that we will also live with him.[54]

"Baptism is an illustration of what actually takes place in our hearts. When you go under the water, it's like being buried—buried with Christ. The old life, the old selfish you, is dead and buried. Coming up out of the water symbolizes that you are rising to a new life, a different life. The old life is dead. A new life in Christ has begun. You're different. You're regenerated. You're changed in heart. You now have Christ living in you, and His spirit in you gives you the grace and power to live for Him. When this new life begins to grow within you, you'll find that you begin to lose your taste for the old life, and you'll have a growing desire to embrace the ways of the Spirit of God."

"It sounds almost too good to be true. Can such a change really take place in me?"

"Yes!" Kyle said emphatically. "This is the good news of the Gospel." He turned to another verse in the Bible and read:

Therefore, if anyone is in Christ, the new creation has come: The old has gone, the new is here! All this is from God, who reconciled us to himself through Christ and gave us the ministry of reconciliation.[55]

I'd been listening to Kyle so intently that I almost forgot we were in a public dining room. Kyle leaned over the table and took my hand.

"Allison, I think the time has come for you to make this decision. Are you willing to let God do this for you? Do you want to leave the old life behind? Do you want to embrace the new life in Jesus Christ?"

"Yes," I said simply. "Yes, I do, but I'm finding it hard to believe that God would do such a thing for me, and I don't know how to do it."

Karen intervened at this point and said, "You know, this is such a vital conversation, and the decision you have to make, Allison, is so important that I know you'll want to think about it. It's so noisy in here with so many distractions. Why don't you both come around to my apartment

---

54 Romans 6:3–8
55 2 Corinthians 5:17–18

tomorrow evening for coffee and we can carry on the talk there. It's quiet and private. We'll not be rushed or disturbed. We can take our time and be sure that we do this right. And you can take your time, Allison, and be sure that this is what you really want to do."

This suggestion pleased me, although I think Kyle would have liked to press the matter further at this moment. When I agreed to Karen's suggestion, Kyle, rather reluctantly, agreed.

"Okay," he said. "Let's make it seven tomorrow night at Karen's place. But in the meantime, Allison, I want you to really think about this. This is the time for you to open your life to God, seek His forgiveness, and ask Him to come into your life and set you on a new path."

I knew Kyle was anxious for me to take this step of trust and commitment to God. I appreciated his concern, but I needed a little more time to think about it. And think about it I did. I found it hard to keep my mind on my studies the rest of the day. I spent the evening alone in my room, thinking about the decision in front of me. *Do I really want to start living God's way? Am I prepared to let go of my old way of life? Would God really change me and make me a new person? Could I really be at peace and harmony with Him in my heart? If I commit myself to live for Him, where will that lead?* I wrestled with these questions all evening. I tried to pray, but I sensed God was waiting for me to make some decisions.

The next day the inner struggle continued. *Should I yield to God? Should I trust Him? Was His way of life really right for me?*

By the time I drove up to Karen's apartment that evening I'd made up my mind. *Yes. I would do it. I would ask Karen and Kyle how to go about it.*

Chapter Seventeen

The Change

Karen lived in a simple two-room apartment. Although small, it was warm and friendly. I was so anxious to solve my spiritual hunger that I was a little impatient when Karen insisted that we have some coffee and refreshments. My spiritual needs felt so intense that I couldn't wait. Before the coffee was finished I said, "I've thought about our conversation yesterday, and I want to give myself to God. I want Him to come into my life and change me, if He'll have me. I want to live differently and have peace and rest in my own heart. I want to be in harmony with Him and live as He wants me to live. So, what do I do from here?"

Kyle laid his half-finished coffee aside, leaned towards me, and said, "You do it by being sure that you repent of the old life. Your willingness to leave it indicates your sincerity. Next you must trust in God. Trust Him to forgive you and change you. Trust Him to give you the new life that will empower you to live for Him. He can do all of that because of what Jesus Christ did for us when He died on the cross and rose again from the dead. If you're ready to do that, then you simply humbly ask Him to do it, and believe that He will answer that prayer."

"You mean we can pray right here?"

"Allison," Kyle said gently, "if you're ready, then God is ready and we can do it right here, right now. Would you like that?"

I could tell that Kyle had this whole thing planned out and thought through, but that didn't discourage me.

"Yes," I said.

"Then let's pray together."

We pulled our chairs into a little circle and knelt to pray.

"You pray, Allison," Kyle said. "Tell God that you've not lived right and you're sorry for this and want to change. Tell Him you need to change what you are in your heart, and you believe that He can do that through Jesus Christ. Then commit yourself to Him and trust His power to come into your life in a new way."

I whispered my prayer, but loud enough for Karen and Kyle to hear what I was saying. I told God how sorry I was for the past. I expressed a desire to change the way I was living, but said I needed His power and grace to forgive me and help me live a new life for Jesus Christ. It seemed such a simple prayer, but as I prayed I was suddenly filled with a wonderful sense of peace and a quiet power such as I'd never felt before. I knew that some transaction had taken place, but I couldn't explain what it was. I felt God was there and that there was harmony between Him and myself. He was part of me; His Spirit was in me. It was so beautiful that I started to sob, but they were tears of relief and tears of joy. I was right with God. I was in touch with Him, and I was overwhelmed by the wonder of it all.

Kyle patiently let some time pass. After a while he gently asked, "Do you believe God heard your prayer, Allison?"

"O yes," I responded. "I know it. I can't explain it or describe it, but I feel different on the inside, and I know that things have changed."

We rose and Karen embraced me and we wept together. Kyle took my hand and said, "Congratulations. You've become a new person in Christ Jesus."

"It's as if a door has closed on the past," I said, "and another door has opened to a whole new way of life."

"It is a new way of life," Kyle said. "Now you must keep on trusting that He has truly done this thing for you. Trust and obey Him and He'll lead you in the way that you should go. Remember that wherever you go, Jesus Christ is in your heart and you are a child of God."

Karen refilled our coffee cups and we sat around to talk.

"Allison," Kyle said, "tonight you started on a new journey with God. Let me mention four things that I think will help you on the journey. First, it will help you if you pray each day. Take time to talk to God and ask for His help and guidance. As you learn to pray, you'll sense His presence more and more, and you'll also begin to understand His voice and what He's saying to you. Second, take time to read the Bible. It's His Word to you, and you'll find guidance, encouragement, and enlightenment in it."

Kyle paused and asked me, "Do you have a Bible, Allison?

I hesitated. "I think so. We should have a family Bible, but I'm not sure where it is."

Karen immediately got up and went into her other room and came back carrying a Bible.

"Here," she said, handing the Bible to me. "I have a number of Bibles, so you can use this one until you get one of your own."

I thanked Karen for this. Then Kyle took up the conversation again.

"Third, find a group of fellow Christians with whom you can fellowship. You'll find encouragement and strength and companionship there. Finally, be prepared to tell others as best you can what God has done for you. Share your faith."

I thanked Kyle and Karen for their help. We sat and talked for a while, and I told them about my father's invitation for lunch after church on Sunday. They were both very happy to know that my father was coming to church, and they were pleased to go out with him after the service.

"Perhaps you should tell your father what has happened to you tonight," Kyle suggested.

I was a little afraid to do this, because I didn't know how my father would react. I always resisted sharing with him any significant private event in my life, but I knew I had to do it, so when I arrived home I asked if we could talk.

"Something important happened to me this evening," I began.

He was immediately interested, so I told him about the conversation with Kyle and Karen. I told him of my prayer that evening in Karen's place and the change I felt in my heart. I concluded by saying, "I've not always been a good daughter to you, Father, but I think God has changed my life and I'll try to be different from now on."

My father sat quietly for a while without responding.

"I'm very glad for you, Allison," he finally said. "I think this is a very important thing that has happened to you. The strange thing is, I believe it's something like this that Jim Dexter and Pastor Lindsey have been saying needs to happen to me. When you're praying, pray for me, too."

This response was very welcome, but was also very different to what I'd anticipated. I didn't know what to say in reply. I'd have to leave it up to the pastor and Jim Dexter to lead my father on from this point. I did, however, promise to pray for him, and I did so as I said my prayers that night.

When I was alone in my room and had time to contemplate what had happened to me, I was deeply aware of a quiet assurance in my heart. A beautiful feeling of peace seemed to be flowing over my soul. I sensed harmony with God. I felt clean. I felt a joy in my inner soul. It was indeed as if I was a new person and new life had come. I remembered to pray and to read my Bible before I went to bed. I noticed my prayers were very different, too. I felt like God was near. I could sense His presence. It was almost as if I could reach out and touch Him. The sense of rightness overwhelmed me. I was in touch with a loving and powerful God. I felt like my hopes were bright and alive. I was ready for a new life and a new direction, and I felt that God knew exactly what that should be. A great river of joy and happiness welled up within me. I knelt for a long time ... not really saying anything ... just letting the waves of this new life roll over me. I slept well that night.

CHAPTER EIGHTEEN

THE TESTIMONY

It felt strange on Sunday morning to be going to church with my father. We journeyed there together, and both Karen and Kyle met us at the church door. We all sat together in the same pew that I had sat in the week before.

The service went very well, but I found that with my new experience of God the content of the service had much more meaning for me. My inner responses to the hymns, prayers, and preaching were much more meaningful. I felt the reality of what was going on, and understood it better because so much of it expressed the experience of my own heart. Throughout the service, however, I kept wondering how my father was reacting to all of this. I knew it would be strange to him, but I hoped it was meaningful and that he understood what was going on. My mind also wandered forward to the lunch that we would have after church. How would we all get on? Would Father like Kyle?

When the service was over I was glad to see Jim Dexter and Carol come over and welcome my father to the church. As they talked I could tell that my father was very comfortable with Jim and enjoyed his company. From what I could understand, my father responded positively to the church service and was glad to have been there. He made a point of thanking Jim for inviting him. I relaxed a little more.

My father took us to a rather expensive restaurant for lunch. It was much grander than we students were used to or could afford. The meal went well. In fact, Kyle and my father seemed to communicate beautifully together. They got talking about engineering and architecture and seemed to speak the same language. Kyle asked about the designs for the new conference centre, and raised questions that indicated he understood and had insight into the whole process. Kyle then got on to the subject of his dream of being able to help churches build suitable buildings that were appropriate and fitted their purposes. His enthusiasm and understanding soon had my father involved. The two of them talked away, leaving Karen and I to our own conversation. My father seemed to be enjoying the experience, and I continued to relax more and more.

On the way home my father commented that he really enjoyed being with me at church and meeting my new friends.

"I really like your new friends, Allison. Kyle seems like a very nice boy with a lot of good ideas and enthusiasm. We'll have to have him come around to the house some time." He looked at me with a smile on his face. "Neither of us are very good cooks, but I'm sure we could rustle up something acceptable for him."

"I'd like that, Dad," I said. The words were out of my mouth before I realized that I had called my father "dad." For years I'd been calling him the more distant and formal "father." It dawned on me that I was feeling closer to him, and that the gulf was being bridged. It seemed quite natural for me to call him the more familiar and intimate name. Things indeed were changing.

The next day Kyle phoned me, which was a new venture for him. He said he had one or two things he wanted to talk to me about.

"First," he said, "I really enjoyed being with your father. I think he's a very fine, knowledgeable, and competent gentleman. He gave me a lot of ideas about church buildings."

I assured Kyle that my dad also enjoyed his company and was impressed with his vision and purpose.

"Allison," Kyle continued, "I think you should tell the Tuesday night group about your experience of accepting God into your life."

I wasn't so sure about that idea.

"It'll be good for you to make a public statement about it," he insisted. "It'll confirm what took place in your own heart, and it'll be a great encouragement to the pastor and the group."

Still I hesitated. "I've never spoken in public about such personal things. I'm not sure I could do it; I may embarrass myself."

"I know you can do it," said Kyle, "and I assure you the group will be very accepting and understanding. Why don't you let me mention it to the pastor so he can introduce you at the beginning of the session? I guarantee you'll get a very accepting and warm reception."

With some reluctance I agreed to do this. My mind immediately began to work on what I would say and how I would say it.

"Just tell the story of what happened," said Kyle, "and then tell of the change that has taken place in your life since then."

I figured that as long as no deep theological understanding or great Bible knowledge was expected, I could simply tell the story of my life and how it had changed since I started coming to the Bible study group. I'd describe how I accepted Jesus into my life and the changes that had taken place since then.

"That'll be great," said Kyle. "Nobody will expect any more than that."

I now looked forward to the Tuesday meeting with some nervousness and trepidation, but in my heart I agreed with Kyle that a public declaration of my new faith would crystallize what had happened to me and commit me to it in a stronger way.

When Tuesday came, the pastor opened the meeting and then said, "Before we start tonight, I believe that Allison has something that she wants to tell us."

I'd given much thought to what I would say and how I whould say it, but I was still apprehensive. Once I got started, however, I found that I was confident and able to express myself to my satisfaction. The group listened intently; some nodded their heads in encouragement as I spoke.

I told them about my early life, that it had not been religious at all. I told them about the death of my mother and the dreadful emptiness that her absence made in my life. I even told of the years of rebellion and wildness, although I made no mention of the abortion or attempted suicide. I explained that I'd lived a very wayward life for a few years, but I now knew that my pleasure seeking was a cover-up to hide the inner emptiness I felt about life and the direction in which I was going. I told about Karen and her friendship and how she invited me to the Bible study group. I expressed to the group my appreciation for their openness in receiving me, and how new hopes and directions had begun to come into my life. I emphasized how the discussions on hope, faith, and love had set me thinking and planning in a whole new direction. Then I told about Kyle and his urgent talk in the university dining room, and then the prayer time in Karen's apartment. I tried to explain how different I felt since then, and the assurance that I was now in harmony with God and the new sense of deep peace I sensed in my heart. This elicited a strong reaction from the group. They began to clap and express encouragement. As I sat down, I felt that this group had accepted me and was supporting me. They understood the experiences that I had gone through.

When I was finished the pastor said, "Isn't that a wonderful story? It's encouraging for us all. I think we all feel like rejoicing and giving God thanks for the change that has come over Allison. When she was talking about the change in her life, my mind went to the hymn that we sometimes sing in church, "Since Jesus Came into My Heart." In fact, I think we should sing it together right now in honour of God and the change He has brought to Allison's life.

Everyone stood and began to sing the hymn with which they were clearly familiar. I didn't know the words, but as I listened I knew they expressed what had happened to me.

> *What a wonderful change in my life has been wrought*
> *Since Jesus come into my heart!*
> *I have light in my soul for which long I had sought,*
> *Since Jesus came into my heart.*
>
> *Since Jesus came into my heart,*
> *Since Jesus came into my heart,*
> *Floods of joy o'er my soul like the sea billows roll,*
> *Since Jesus came into my heart.*
>
> *I have ceased from my wand'ring and going astray,*
> *Since Jesus came into my heart.*
> *And my sins which were many are all washed away,*
> *Since Jesus come into my heart.*[56]

They sang with enthusiasm, and when the song was finished they all clapped again. It was a very joyful time, and I felt accepted and part of the group.

---

56 *Since Jesus Came into my Heart*, Rufus H. McDaniel (1914)

CHAPTER NINETEEN

THE REALITY

When things had settled down, the pastor began his presentation. "We rejoice with Allison over her new life," the pastor began. "In fact, Allison's story and what she has described is a good illustration of the power of the dynamic trio and how God uses these qualities to influence our lives and lead us to Him. For Allison, they brought new hope and purpose in the midst of her discouragements. She began to accept these hopes, and then in faith she began to undertake what was necessary to make them a reality. She also understood that the power of divine love was absent in her life, and she could never live the way she wanted to unless God came into her life with His love, forgiveness, and strength. It's a good illustration of God at work through hope, faith, and love."

Many in the group nodded their heads in agreement. Referring to his notes, the pastor went on.

"Last week we talked about love as the lead singer in the trio. It's God's love, and only He can bring it into our lives. If He doesn't give it, we don't have it. When this love is flowing in our hearts, things begin to happen. It's this love that purifies the motivations for our hopes and faith. It's the intensity of this love that creates strong hopes and faith. It's this love for God and others that gives us strength to keep pursuing our hopes with faith, even when circumstances, events, or people are discouraging and difficult. It's this love that gives us the determination to keep on course when we realize that the fulfillment of our dreams calls for great sacrifice and commitment. It's also this love in our hearts that distinguishes us as Christians. We love things that others don't love, and we don't love what many others do love. In addition to all of this, it's our love for God that fills us with His peace and joy and gives us the wonder of harmonizing our wills with His."

The pastor looked up and smiled at us. "That's quite a list of things love does for us," he said, "but there's even more. This love is a powerful, life changing, character-transforming thing. Let me point out one or two other things that this love of God will bring into our lives.

"First, I want you to note the abundance of this love. There is no short-age here at all, which is why Paul says, *"... and hope does not put us to shame, because God's love has been poured out into our hearts through the Holy Spirit, who has been given to us."*[57] God wants to pour His love into us. It comes from an infinite reservoir. It's an endless ocean. No drops and dribbles here—it is poured out. There is abundance. It comes in streams that will never run dry. No matter how empty we are, our hearts can be filled with the wonder-ful warmth and power of the love of God. There's enough to help us love everyone—even those we find hard to love. There's so much love that there's even enough for us to love our enemies. That's why Jesus could tell us to *"... love your enemies and pray for those who persecute you."*[58] By ourselves we don't have love enough to do that, but when the love of God is poured into our hearts, it is so abundant that there's enough for us to love our enemies and those, who by nature, we would not like or love. The hymn-writer gave a vivid word picture of the abundance of God's love when he wrote:

> *Could we with ink the ocean fill,*
> *And were the skies of parchment made,*
> *Were ev'ry stock on earth a quill,*
> *And ev'ry man a scribe by trade,*
> *To write the love of God above*
> *Would drain the ocean dry;*
> *Nor could the scroll contain the whole,*
> *Tho' stretched from sky to sky.*[59]

"It is an abundant love. When this warm and strong love of God is flow-ing in your life, you will live life to the full. It will be an abundant life. No wonder Jesus said, *"I have come that they may have life, and have it to the full."*[60]

---

57 Romans 5:5
58 Matthew 5:44
59 *The Love of God*, Frederick M. Lehman (1917)
60 John 10:10

Kyle inserted a thought at this point. "When you describe the importance of love like this, it makes me think that it was really for this purpose that we were first created and formed. We were made to have a loving relationship with God. There's no way that we'll ever be truly satisfied in heart and soul until we are in loving harmony with Him. This is what we are made for. Our nature and our spiritual makeup are such that we'll never be truly satisfied until we're in loving relationship with God. This is the home of the soul. This is what we long for and hunger for, and only in this will we really be satisfied."

"Yes," said the pastor, "when God created man in the beginning, He created us in his own image. Humanity was given a living soul. If we're a living soul made in the image of God, then what we're made for is to enjoy this wonderful experience of being filled with His presence and living in harmony and fellowship with the God of love."

Another man, John, who had not yet spoken in any of the meetings I had been to now spoke up and said, "I work with tools all the time. I think this is like making a tool. A tool is manufactured for a particular purpose and use. When a tool is used for what it was made to do, then it's effective and productive, but when you try to use it for jobs that it wasn't built for, it becomes awkward and useless. A hammer is good for pounding nails. Saws are manufactured to cut wood, and they do this very well. But have you ever tried to pound nails with a saw, or cut wood with a hammer?"

We all smiled at this simple, yet vivid, illustration.

John went on. "Tools are clumsy and inefficient when they're used for purposes they weren't made to perform. We were made and created to live in harmony and fellowship with God, and we function best when we do what we were made to do. We'll never be truly satisfied or find our true purpose until we learn to love and obey Him."

"Right," another person exclaimed. "I was thinking the same thing. All of the other things that we enjoy and participate in, and that we hope will give us ultimate happiness and satisfaction, may be fine and good in their place, but they'll never be quite enough to fill and satisfy the soul. It's a loving relationship with God that brings joy, peace, and fulfillment to our hearts."

"You are absolutely correct in this," said the pastor. "The human spirit will be forever restless until it finds its rest in Him. There are many pleasures and enjoyments that we should participate in, but ultimately the greatest joy is in a loving relationship with God. I think Bernard of Clair-vaux voiced it well when he wrote:

Jesus Thou Joy of loving hearts,
Thou Fount of life, Thou Light of men,
From the best bliss that earth imparts
We turn unfilled to Thee again.

Never in all of my life have I ever thought in terms of fellowship with God as the ultimate in human experience, joy and satisfaction. I'm being introduced to so many new and exciting thoughts.

The pastor continued his presentation. "You can begin to see why Jesus placed love at the centre of our Christian experience. So much revolves around it. In fact, love is the hub from which all kinds of other benefits and blessings radiate. Let me change the illustration. When you get medication from the doctor and read the instructions you find that most medicines have side-effects. While many drugs are designed to help you with your ailments, you must also be aware that they may affect you in other ways that extend beyond their primary purpose. Medicines can have side effects that sometimes are quite unexpected. Well, love is like a great medicine for the soul, and it brings with it a lot of side effects. But the side effects of love are good and healthy and pleasant. Love reaches into all aspects of life and living. The Apostle Paul gives a list of things that he calls the fruit of the Spirit. The first and most important on the list is love. The others flow from love, just like the side effects of medicine, but what a beautiful list they are:

'But the fruit of the Spirit is love, joy, peace, forbearance, kindness, goodness, faithfulness, gentleness and self-control.'[61]

"Those are the welcome side effects of love. Love is a many-faceted thing. It brings with it many companions. It influences every aspect of our lives and our personalities. Paul calls them the fruit of the Spirit because a loving relationship with God is the fertile ground in the human heart from which grows a beautiful and fruitful harvest. Love in the heart blossoms into many different beautiful flowers. It matures all aspects of our personality and our relationships with others. Paul describes it well when he says:

61 Galatians 5:22–23

Love is patient, love is kind. It does not envy, it does not boast, it is not proud. It does not dishonor others, it is not self-seeking, it is not easily angered, it keeps no record of wrongs. Love does not delight in evil but rejoices with the truth. It always protects, always trusts, always hopes, always perseveres. Love never fails...[62]

"You can see from this wonderful passage of scripture that the presence of divine love in the heart brings all kinds of positive side effects. But still there's more. Divine love becomes the dynamo that generates within us the true spirit of holiness. The Bible is constantly urging us as followers of Jesus to be holy in our living, in our attitudes, and in our values. Holiness of heart and life should be characteristic of God's people. God is holy, so if His Spirit lives within us, then we should begin to reflect this holiness. The Apostle Peter states that principle clearly when he said to the early Christians: *'But just as he who called you is holy, so be holy in all you do; for it is written: Be holy, because I am holy.'*[63]

Paul presses the same issue when he says:

I urge you, brothers and sisters, in view of God's mercy, to offer your bodies as a living sacrifice, holy and pleasing to God—this is your true and proper worship. Do not conform to the pattern of this world, but be transformed by the renewing of your mind. Then you will be able to test and approve what God's will is—his good, pleasing and perfect will.[64]

This seems to make so much sense to me, I thought. *Why have I never dealt with any of these issues in my lifetime? Where have I been?*

The pastor continued. "Some people have a mistaken idea of what holiness is really like. They don't think of holiness as a very appealing thing. In fact, they think of it as mostly negative. Holiness to them is primarily a list of things that they must not do. It's a set of very demanding rules. If we're really holy, we keep all of the rules. This view of the holy life can become very legalistic and foster a self-righteousness and judgmental spirit. It can become brittle and harsh."

---

62 1 Corinthians 13:4–8
63 1 Peter 1:15–16
64 Romans 12:1–2

"Wasn't that the problem that the Scribes and Pharisees had in Jesus' time?" someone asked. "They had an extensive set of very strict rules, and they believed that if you were holy you kept the rules and conformed to them. To break the rules was to be unholy. Jesus pointed out to them that while they worked hard at trying to keep all of the rules, they were often unrighteous in the secret attitudes and motives of their hearts."

"Yes," agreed the pastor, "and Jesus was very stern in His rejection of this type of holiness. In very strong language he said:

Woe to you, teachers of the law and Pharisees, you hypocrites! You clean the outside of the cup and dish, but inside they are full of greed and self-indulgence. Blind Pharisees! First clean the inside of the cup and dish, and then the outside also will be clean.[65]

One young lady interjected her thoughts at this time with considerable emotion. "This kind of Christianity almost destroyed me. The people in the church I went to kept on burdening me with all kinds of rules that made little sense to me, but they made it clear that if I broke any of the rules, I wasn't a good Christian. I was often scolded for not being committed enough. But in the midst of all of the judgments, they exhibited very little warmth, care, or love. It was all so very brittle. It almost turned me against Christianity until a good friend pointed out to me that Jesus didn't want this kind of Christianity either."

I noticed that a number of the group nodded in support of this statement.

The pastor responded. "Jesus made it clear that this kind of holiness was quite foreign to the holiness of heart and life that He was encouraging. He said plainly that the righteousness of the Scribes and Pharisees was empty, dead, and killing. He pointed out that you could keep all of the rules and yet be sour, judgmental, bitter, and self-righteous. Listen to His words: '*For I tell you that unless your righteousness surpasses that of the Pharisees and the teachers of the law, you will certainly not enter the kingdom of heaven.*'[66]

To Jesus, holiness of heart and life was not the dry, killing demands of keeping a set of rules, but rather a living, dynamic, life-giving experience of loving God and others. It's the holiness that comes from the free flow of

---

65 Matthew 22:25–26
66 Matthew 5:20

the love of God within our hearts. It's not a set of rules; it's an atmosphere, an attitude.

"Now don't misunderstand me," emphasized the pastor. "Holiness has two sides to it. It has a negative side, in which you refrain from evil. You reject the spirit of selfishness, sin, and bad attitudes in the heart. You reject any habit or action that's contrary to the will of God. But holiness is also a positive thing. Your heart is filled with the warm love of God. You are motivated by a spirit of caring for others and a spirit of reverence and humble obedience to God. It urges you to do good, and to serve God and others.

"Holiness implies the absence of hurtful and poisonous attitudes. When love rules in your heart, hatred, spite, jealously, and envy are banished. When you're full of God's love, there is no place for selfishness, greed, and self-will. Love not only brings great benefits into our lives, but it also banishes the sinful and selfish elements that bring discord and disharmony between God and us, and between other people and us. A holy life is not so much something that we try hard to attain with great discipline and effort, but it's the natural outcome of the attitudes and values that exist in the heart that is in a loving relationship with God."

"So," said Kyle, thinking again in his engineering terms, "if we're going to build a Christian life that is worthy and in the beauty of holiness, then that life is built on the foundation of our love for God."

"Yes," said the pastor. "No true holiness can exist where there is a lack of love. That's why Jesus gave absolute priority to love. I've quoted it before, but I'll quote it again to you. Jesus said the first and most important commandment is to:

> *Love the Lord your God with all your heart and with all your soul and with your entire mind. This is the first and greatest commandment. And the second is like it: "Love your neighbor as yourself." All the Law and the Prophets hang on these two commandments.*[67]

"When the heart is full of love like this, then it is clean. There is freedom from unloving attitudes or feelings. Love and sinful selfishness cannot live together in peace in the same heart. One will seek to destroy the other.

---

67 Matthew 22:37–40

"Remember that we're talking about a dynamic trio here—hope, faith, and love. They support one another and build one another. Love generates hope and faith, and hope and faith encourage love."

After he said this, the pastor sat back and announced to us, "I have one other important thing to say about love, but this last point is so important that I'd like to leave it until after we have a break and relax a little."

During the break we helped ourselves to some coffee, and then Karen, Kyle, and I sat down comfortably on our chesterfield. As we drank our coffee we talked things over.

"This is a little overwhelming for me," I admitted. "There are issues here that I've never dealt with. In my previous life, these concerns never surfaced. Will I ever be able to handle all of this new thinking and new experiences?"

"What's being said tonight is important for all of us. It certainly gets to the heart of things, doesn't it?" said Kyle.

As we were talking about this, Jim Dexter came over and joined our group.

"Allison, thank you for your testimony tonight. It was a great encouragement to me and to the whole group. I hope you'll find help and direction for your new Christian life from our fellowship. Certainly if I can ever be of help, I want you to feel free to come to me."

I thanked Jim for this gracious offer. He then asked, "Did your father enjoy church on Sunday morning?"

"Yes," I responded. "I think he was very impressed with it. He seems to have appreciated not only the church, but also the conversations he's been having with you and Pastor Lindsey. He respects both of you."

"I'm glad to hear that," said Jim. "Carol and I are thinking of having him come over to our house for supper one night. Do you think it would be alright for us to invite him?"

"Certainly," I replied. "He's very busy these days with the new conference centre, so I've been doing a lot of the cooking. I think he'd appreciate a decent meal for a change."

Jim smiled. "We would love to have you come sometime as well, but I feel as if your father has things he wants to deal with, and this time he'd be more comfortable if you weren't there. Would you be offended if we invited just him this time around?"

I was a little surprised to hear that my dad was exhibiting so much interest in spiritual things, but I was also very glad.

"Of course," I assured him. "That would be the correct thing to do. Don't worry about me. I can always go out and get something to eat."

"We also thought it would be good if the pastor came for the meal as well. Do you think it would be wise to have him come?"

"My dad is very impressed with the pastor. He respects him, and I think he'd listen to him, so I believe it would add a great deal if the pastor was there."

"Good," said Jim. "I'll call your father and make arrangements."

Jim moved on to speak to some others.

"When they decide on which night they'll have the supper," Kyle said, "let me take you out that night for something to eat. I'd hate for you to get food poisoning from your own cooking."

I was secretly delighted with this offer, but tried to sound only moderately pleased when I accepted Kyle's invitation and thanked him for his kindness. Kyle then invited Karen to join us, but Karen sensitively declined.

I was also very encouraged by the number of people who came over to me during the coffee break and expressed their happiness over the testimony I gave that night. Their approval and support helped confirm in my mind the reality of what had happened to me.

"Now," said the pastor when the coffee break was over, " I want to talk to you about the ultimate objective of love. We are constantly urged to love God with all of our hearts, and love our neighbour as ourselves. This experience of inner love leads us to the ultimate in spiritual experience. It unites us to God in such a way that God lives in us and we live in Him. What greater objective can be imagined than this? To be in such a state of harmony with God, to be so aware of His presence and love in our hearts that we are united with Him so that He lives in us and we live in Him. This is the ultimate spiritual reality. This is a spiritual state of such harmony with God that we love what He loves, value what He values, and desire what He desires. He lives in us and expresses Himself through us. When we talk about hope and faith, this should become our greatest hope and our final faith—oneness with God.

"Paul describes this intimate relationship with God as a great spiritual mystery that has now been revealed. He said:

The mystery that has been kept hidden for ages and generations, but is now disclosed to the Lord's people. To them God has chosen to make known among the Gentiles the glorious riches of this mystery, which is Christ in you, the hope of glory.[68]

"The ultimate glory, the final reality is Christ in us. This is our central objective and goal. Since God is a God of holy love, this inner harmony with Him can only happen when the soul is bathed in His love and filled with His spirit of holiness. While all of us have many hopes that we should pursue and develop, this should be the ultimate—that we become joined to Him in holy love so that He is in us and we are in Him.

"Paul expressed the great hope and dream of his life when he said: '... *I consider everything a loss compared to the surpassing worth of knowing Christ Jesus my Lord, for whose sake I have lost all things ...*'[69]

"He goes on to explain the great objective of his spiritual life:

I want to know Christ—yes, to know the power of his resurrection and participation in his sufferings, becoming like him in his death, and so, somehow, to attain to the resurrection from the dead.[70]

"The dominant hope, the strongest faith, is focused on this great spiritual aspiration of knowing Christ in a close and intimate fellowship. Love is the quality that makes this relationship a reality.

"Jesus went so far as to indicate that the bonds of love can bind us so close to God that our relationship with God is like His own relationship with God the Father. Jesus made an amazing statement to the disciples as He was preparing to leave them:

On that day you will realize that I am in my Father, and you are in me, and I am in you. Whoever has my commands and keeps them is the one who loves me. The one who loves me will be loved by my Father, and I too will love him and show myself to him.[71]

---

68 Colossians 1:26–27
69 Philippians 3:8
70 Philippians 3:10–11
71 John 14:20–21

"He goes on to say: '*Anyone who loves me will obey my teaching. My Father will love them, and we will come to them and make our home with them.*'[72]

"When we are governed by the spirit of holy love, God is at home in our hearts.

"In His great prayer at the end of His life, Jesus prayed for His followers and expressed His great desire for them. He prayed for us:

That all of them may be one, Father, just as you are in me and I am in you. May they also be in us so that the world may believe that you have sent me.[73]

"This is the power of love, that God will live in us and be one with us, just as He and Jesus live together. It's a relationship of love. It thrives on love. It dies if love dies.

"In his epistles, John explains that this love between God and us also expresses itself in our love for each other. He says:

Dear friends, let us love one another, for love comes from God. Everyone who loves has been born of God and knows God. Whoever does not love does not know God, because God is love.[74]

"John concludes with: '*God is love. Whoever lives in love lives in God, and God in him.*'[75] This conscious, harmonious, rich relationship with God is the ultimate goal of our searching soul. This experience of love should be our dominant hope and the final goal of our faith."

The pastor closed his Bible, sat back, and said, "This ends the series on hope and faith and love—the dynamic trio." Pastor Lindsey looked at us all and then with great affection in his voice continued. "You have many things for which you hope. Many of these hopes will harmonize with God's will for your life, and I encourage you to pursue these hopes. But in all of your hoping, my prayer is that above all things you will hope for this loving, harmonious relationship with God, so that He dwells in you and you in Him. This is the greatest hope. This is the ultimate reality. You should hope

---

72 John 14:23
73 John 17:21
74 1 John 4:7–8
75 1 John 4:16(b)

for this above all else. I also urge you to realize your hopes by putting your faith to work. I trust that you will especially work and labour to make this hope real in your life, and that you'll apply your faith to this great objective—to love God with all your heart and to love your neighbour as yourself. In all of your seeking, seek this. In all of your striving, strive for this. '*And now these three remain: faith, hope and love. But the greatest of these is love.*'[76]

"In conclusion," said the pastor, "I'd like to tell you that my prayer for you all is like the prayer that Paul prayed for the Christians in Ephesus:

> *I pray that out of his glorious riches he may strengthen you with power through his Spirit in your inner being, so that Christ may dwell in your hearts through faith. And I pray that you, being rooted and established in love, may have power, together with all the Lord's holy people, to grasp how wide and long and high and deep is the love of Christ, and to know this love that surpasses knowledge— that you may be filled to the measure of all the fullness of God.*[77]

"Amen."

A solemn stillness pervaded the room as we all sat and tried to absorb what the pastor had said. We were aware of the truth of his message, and it seemed that there was a Presence in the room that endorsed that truth and was making it all very vivid to us.

After a few minutes of quietness, the pastor turned to Jim Dexter and indicated that he should take over the meeting.

Jim took time to express our thanks to the pastor for coming to our gathering and sharing with us all of his rich understanding about hope, faith, and love. The whole group, without prompting, stood and applauded in a spontaneous show of appreciation. It was heartfelt thanks for what we'd learned from this man. I couldn't help but compare how different my life was now at the end of this series to how it had been at the start. I knew that I was entirely different, and I thanked God and also the friends and helpers in this group for being with me through the changes.

---

76 1 Corinthians 13:13
77 Ephesians 3:16–19

CHAPTER TWENTY

THE JOY

The changes in my life were not finished yet. I knew I had to put my faith into action, so the next day I went to the guidance counsellor at the university to inquire about changing my course selection so that I could get into counselling as a career. When I had a good understanding of what was involved in this change, I spoke to my father, since he was helping me through university with the finances. He was most encouraging and felt this was the right move for me. I decided to change directions at the end of this term and find the proper training to begin my preparation for a life of counselling.

Jim and Carol Dexter didn't waste any time in making contact with my father. They invited him over for supper on Thursday evening, and the pastor was there as well. Kyle kept his commitment to me, and we went out for supper that evening. I enjoyed the evening thoroughly, and I felt the bond between Kyle and I growing stronger. We didn't hurry through the evening, and it was rather late when I got home. I was a little surprised to find that my father had not yet returned from the Dexter's. I waited up for him. I was anxious to hear how the supper meeting went. I waited until it was very late and he still hadn't returned. Finally I went to bed. I'd been in bed for some time when I heard the car drive into the driveway and my father come into the house.

I was surprised when I heard a knock at my bedroom door and my father's voice saying, "Allison, are you sleeping?"

"No, come in and tell me how you got on."

My father came in and sat on the bed. "Allison, I've had a wonderful night. You told me about the experience you had in Karen's apartment when you prayed with Kyle and Karen, and it seemed to you that God came into your life and everything was changed."

I nodded in agreement.

"Well, I've had a similar experience tonight with the Dexter's and the pastor. My life has been busy and full, and I've not made much time for God. The truth is, I haven't really been interested; I thought I could handle life myself without any help from Him. I've neglected Him and rejected the idea that He could have an important role to play in my living. I was wrong in that, Allison, and tonight I prayed that God would forgive me for my self-indulgent living and that He would come into my life. I believe He heard that prayer and has changed me. I want to live by faith in Him and trust His way of life."

I reached out and took my father's hand, but could say nothing because tears were running down my cheeks. But he knew, without words, that my heart was full.

"Allison, I've not been a good father to you as far as helping you with your spiritual life. I'll try now to do better. Could we start right now and try to pray together?"

Still unable to speak, I nodded, and my father and I bowed together and for the first time that I can remember, prayed together. His prayer was simple and unpretentious. He prayed that God would forgive him for his neglect of my spiritual welfare, and that God would help us do better in the future. He then kissed my cheek and left me to my thoughts. I wondered what the impact of this would be in our lives.

My father and I went together to church again on Sunday. Kyle and Karen were waiting for us on the steps of the church. Dad said that he would let me off at the door and then go and find an empty spot in the already crowded parking lot. I stood with Kyle and Karen on the front steps waiting for Dad to come. As I stood there with my two dear friends and watched my father walk from the parking lot towards the church steps, I was suddenly overwhelmed with a surprising sense of happiness. Sheer joy gripped me beyond anything I'd ever experienced in my life before. It rolled over me like a great swelling tide. When my father reached us, Karen took his arm and walked into the church with him. I took Kyle's arm and we followed. My heart was singing; my soul was delighted. I went into church to worship the great God—the God of hope, the God of faith, the God of love—especially the God of love.

Also by Bill Stewart

Journey into Prayer
Journey into Holiness
Journey into Wisdom

To order, contact the author at
stewartw@rogers.com